"We did not see you all of the sudden," L'as'wa said, then pointed to the others standing behind her. "We thought you disappeared."

"No, but someone else did," Kathryn said. "I was just going to see where she went," she added, turning the doorknob.

The door swung open slowly. Kathryn was in the lead, with the four cadets following close behind.

Fixtures along the ceiling bathed the room in a bright yellow light.

"I just want to find out if I'm going crazy," explained Kathryn, shading her eyes and looking around the empty room. "Plus, if I can learn anything about the air outside the domes, I'd—"

Before Kathryn finished her sentence, the door they entered slammed shut. Just as suddenly, alarms started chiming and ringing. She dropped her tricorder and covered her ears to shut out the noise. The instrument bounced across the room. As Kathryn watched in dismay, a thick metal plate slid over the exit—crushing the tricorder under its weight!

Then suddenly, the lights went out.

And even though the alarms still blared, Kathryn could hear Mari's voice.

"We're trapped!"

Available from MINSTREL Books

STAR TREK®
VOYAGER™

STARFLEET ACADEMY®

QUARANTINE

Patricia Barnes-Svarney

Interior Illustrations by
Jason Palmer

A
MINSTREL®
BOOK

Published by POCKET BOOKS
New York   London   Toronto   Sydney   Tokyo   Singapore

A MINSTREL PAPERBACK *Original*

A Minstrel Book published by
POCKET BOOKS, a division of Simon & Schuster Inc.
1230 Avenue of the Americas, New York, NY 10020

Copyright © 1997 by Paramount Pictures. All Rights Reserved.

STAR TREK is a registered trademark of Paramount Pictures.

A VIACOM COMPANY

This book is published by Pocket Books, a division of Simon & Schuster Inc., under exclusive license from Paramount Pictures.

ISBN: 0-671-00733-5

First Minstrel Books printing October 1997

10 9 8 7 6 5 4 3 2 1

A MINSTREL BOOK and colophon are registered trademarks of Simon & Schuster Inc.

Cover art by Michael Herring

Printed in the U.S.A.

Again, as always, to Helen, Billy, and the Bear

STARFLEET TIMELINE

2264

The launch of Captain James T. Kirk's five-year mission, _U.S.S. Enterprise,_ NCC-1701.

2292

Alliance between the Klingon Empire and the Romulan Star Empire collapses.

2293

Colonel Worf, grandfather of Worf Rozhenko, defends Captain Kirk and Doctor McCoy at their trial for the murder of Klingon chancellor Gorkon.

Khitomer Peace Conference, Klingon Empire/Federation (_Star Trek VI_).

2323

Jean-Luc Picard enters Starfleet Academy's standard four-year program.

2328

The Cardassian Empire annexes the Bajoran homeworld.

2346

Romulan massacre of Klingon outpost on Khitomer.

2351

In orbit around Bajor, the Cardassians construct a space station that they will later abandon.

2353

Kathryn Janeway enters Starfleet Academy.

2355

Kathryn Janeway meets Admiral Paris and begins a lifelong association with the esteemed scientist.

2363

Captain Jean-Luc Picard assumes command of U.S.S. Enterprise, NCC-1701-D

2367

Wesley Crusher enters Starfleet Academy.

An uneasy truce is signed between the Cardassians and the Federation.

Borg attack at Wolf 359; First Officer Lieutenant Commander Benjamin Sisko and his son, Jake, are among the survivors.

U.S.S. Enterprise-D defeats the Borg vessel in orbit around Earth.

2369

Commander Benjamin Sisko assumes command of Deep Space Nine in orbit over Bajor.

2371

U.S.S. Enterprise, NCC-1701-D, destroyed on Veridian III.

Former Enterprise captain James T. Kirk emerges from a temporal nexus, but dies helping Picard save the Veridian system.

U.S.S. Voyager, under the command of Captain Kathryn Janeway, is accidentally transported to the Delta Quadrant. The crew begins a 70-year journey back to Federation space.

2372

The Klingon Empire's attempted invasion of Cardassia Prime results in the dissolution of the Khitomer peace treaty between the Federation and the Klingon Empire.

Source: Star Trek® Chronology / Michael Okuda and Denise Okuda and Star Trek® Voyager™ Mosaic/Jeri Taylor

QUARANTINE

Chapter

1

*"Psssttt—*Kathryn!"

Kathryn Janeway jumped in her seat. Embarrassed to be caught not paying attention, she blushed and turned to the cadet sitting one empty seat away from her. "What?" she said, trying not to sound too frazzled— then smiled when she realized who had called her name. "Oh, Geordi—hi."

"Here's the data you asked for yesterday on the geologic instability of Prembrose Four," said Geordi La Forge, reaching over and passing a yellow data disk to Kathryn. Like Kathryn, Geordi was a first-year cadet and was in several of her classes. And he just happened to have a knack for finding the most obscure information from the most amazing sources. "Just hypertext the words *mega-volcanic activity*. There are tons of references to the event."

Kathryn reached for the data disk. "You're a lifesaver, Geordi—thanks. How did you find all this information so quickly? Someday, you'll have to show me how you do it."

"Ha! That'll be the day," he said, running his hand through his short, dark hair. "That little secret may be my ticket to making it through Starfleet Academy. That is, if I can make it through gym class."

Kathryn chuckled. "Really, thanks, Geordi. I'll check it over and get it back to you," she hesitated, ". . . as soon as I can."

"No hurry," Geordi answered. "I just wanted to make sure you had it before I forgot to give it to you. Did that make sense?" Kathryn sometimes didn't know if Geordi was joking or not. He wore a VISOR—Visual Instrument and Sensory Organ Replacement—a metal device that wrapped around half of his head and covered his eyes. Blind since birth, Geordi needed the VISOR to see the world around him. Kathryn knew enough about VISOR technology to know that Geordi could "see" the full electromagnetic spectrum. He could interpret objects at different wavelengths—from the infrared to the ultraviolet—in other words, in ways that Kathryn couldn't see.

"Don't worry," she said, still smiling at the cadet. "Nothing makes too much sense to me today anyway." She stuffed the disk into her jumpsuit pocket and turned her attention to the front of the large auditorium. Timothy Wang, a friend of Kathryn's and a first-year cadet in several of her classes, was poised at the podium, beginning his lecture on the fluid dynamics of space shuttles in a thin atmosphere.

She concentrated on Timothy's lecture, but for only a few minutes. Then she began to squirm in her seat. She really tried to listen to his lecture, not only because she was interested in shuttle design, but she would also have to give a lecture in front of the class—a requirement for this Systems Dynamics course. But her mind was definitely somewhere else.

In fact, my mind is so far removed from this auditorium that I might as well be on Saturn, she thought.

Kathryn knew very well why her mind was elsewhere. She and four other cadets—Timothy, Mari Lakoo, Blinar, and L'as'wa Ranna—had been chosen for a routine mission on the starship *U.S.S. Tsiolkovsky* to the planet Chatoob. It was a chance Kathryn would not have given up for anything. Finally, she would travel to another world.

Of course, she had traveled to other planets within the solar system. When she was nine years old, her father took her to the Mars Colony as a special treat, while he worked on examining the Colony's defense systems. Their travels took them to Starfleet Headquarters in San Francisco, then on the shuttle *Curie* to Mars. She asked dozens of questions of the shuttle pilot, Cadet Data, the first sentient android in Starfleet Academy—or in the Federation, for that matter. And his answers to her many questions confirmed what she began to know: She, too, wanted to join Starfleet Academy. Later, after her father became a Starfleet vice admiral and had many duties on the red planet, her family visited Mars quite often.

But Chatoob was different. It was a planet far beyond the realm of the solar system—light-years away from the Sun, even farther than the small belt of rocky asteroid-like objects that orbited just beyond the planet Pluto. Chatoob was at least nine light-years away from Earth—far enough to employ the services of an Oberth-class starship.

Starfleet Academy often chose a small number of first-year cadets to travel with starships on brief missions—as Kathryn's friend Timothy called it—a kind of "beginner's guide to starships." This time, Kathryn and the others were assigned to the science ship, the *Tsiolkovsky*. The mission was not complicated: The ship would deliver medical equipment to the planet—with several Starfleet doctors demonstrating the technology—while the captain would negotiate with the Chatoob government to possibly join the Federation. The ship would then head back for Earth, beam the Academy cadets back to Paris, and continue on its next mission.

While onboard, each cadet would be assigned a bridge officer, in order to understand how each officer handles his or her tasks and especially to see what it's like to work as a team on a starship. Kathryn was particularly excited about her assignment: The *Tsiolkovsky*'s Chief Science Officer Emma Tapper was to be her reporting officer.

Kathryn wiggled again in her seat. Deep down inside, she wondered if she would do well—or if she would make a complete fool of herself. *If I bit my nails, I'd be doing it right now,* she thought. *Then again, maybe I should start?* She shook her head, chuckling at her nervousness.

As Timothy began to point to a three-dimensional drawing of a shuttle entering orbit, Kathryn let out a deep sigh. Geordi La Forge leaned toward her and smiled. "Are you all right, Cadet?" he whispered.

Kathryn nodded and smiled back. Geordi leaned closer to her. "I bet you're going on the *Tsiolkovsky* mission."

She stared at him, wide-eyed—then squinted. "And why do you say that?"

Geordi chuckled. "Oh, I don't know. But just by looking around this room, I'd say . . . let's see," he said, turning his head to look around the auditorium. "I bet L'as'wa Ranna's going—and I bet Mari Lakoo, too."

"But how—why do you say that?" she whispered urgently, intrigued to find out how Geordi knew. "The list of the cadets going on the *Tsiolkovsky*'s mission is confidential until about a half hour after this class. The chosen cadets are the only ones who know and they're sworn to secrecy."

"Easy," he said, still whispering. He pointed to his VISOR. "I can see in the infrared. When someone is really, really nervous—just like I would be if I were going on a mission—I see a brightening in the infrared through my VISOR. The bright red coloring I 'see' is the excessive amount of heat you're putting out. And of all the first-year cadets in this room, you and the other two cadets have the brightest red coloring from the central nervous system. So does Timothy, but he's giving a lecture, so I really can't tell. I get nervous when I give a lecture, too."

Kathryn was about to tell Geordi that Timothy was also on the list, but then thought he would find out soon enough. She looked at Geordi, amazed. "You can see all that with your VISOR?"

Geordi nodded. "It doesn't always work, but I was just betting that was why the infrared readings from you were high. For all I knew, you all could have just come from gym class. That hikes up the infrared, too."

"I guess I'd better watch my nervous system when I'm around you," Kathryn noted. She tilted her head and whispered, "But I have an even better observation, Geordi. I know you weren't on the list. Why aren't you going on this mission? Certainly you would qualify."

Geordi shook his head. "Oh, yeah. I really wish I could go. But I have another commitment called the Academy Band."

"You're in the band?"

"Well, in a way. I'm the roadie," he said, beaming. "I take care of all the setting up and tearing down of the gear—for practice and performances—and all sorts of things. When they travel, I travel, and we've already been off-world. We're practicing for that big ambassador's conference next week at Starfleet Headquarters. We're the entertainment."

The bell for the end of class sounded just as Kathryn was about to answer.

"I'd better get going or I'll be late for practice. Good luck!" Geordi said, grabbing his padds and running for the exit.

Nodding to Geordi and collecting her padds, Kathryn looked up to see Timothy waving at her from the front of the auditorium. She gave him a weak smile and waved back, feeling guilty. She had not paid attention to a word Timothy said during his entire speech. Then again, she had a feeling the other cadets going on the *Tsiolkovsky* had the same problem.

Kathryn raced from the auditorium, juggling her assignment and duty padds. She had only an hour to get back to the dorm, finish packing, and race for the shuttle. She knew that the student shuttle—in which cadets practiced flying shuttles short distances inside the earth's atmosphere—wouldn't wait for her or the other cadets if they were late. Today's practice flight would take the cadets and some medical equipment to Paris, where they would beam up to the *Tsiolkovsky*. Not only that, she was anxious to contact her parents to tell them the news. She couldn't wait to see the look on her father's face as she told him about her first opportunity to work on a starship bridge. And she could imagine him praising her for a job well-done.

Still trying to balance the numerous data padds in her left arm, Kathryn was suddenly outside on the Academy grounds. The breeze blowing in from the Pacific Ocean was refreshing. For a moment, she took a deep breath of air and thought about the beauty and history surrounding her. There were the old trees of the Academy—some of the oldest stands in San Francisco. Colorful birds flew from tree to tree, the result of the Academy grounds being designated a bird sanctuary for more than a century. And there were the long gravel

pathways along which legendary cadets—such as starship
Captain James T. Kirk, and ambassador to many worlds,
Greffrum Kartz—once walked.

Snap out of it, Kathryn, she thought. *Stick to the task
at hand.*

Finally maintaining some kind of balance with her
padds, Kathryn looked around and took the straightest
route—right through a patch of bright, colorful flowers.

"Hey, watch what you're doing! You're stepping on
the pachysandra!"

Kathryn stopped short and saw an older man waving
a small spade. His pants were soiled on the knees and
his hands were dark with dirt. Kathryn had heard stories
about this man—the Academy groundskeeper, Mr.
Boothby. She swallowed hard and peered over the data
padds. "I'm . . . I'm sorry, sir. But I'm really in a hurry.
I have some important things to do, you know, so—"

Boothby held up a hand and Kathryn stopped talking
immediately. "In a hurry, eh? In too much of a hurry to
watch what you're doing?"

"Well, I—"

"You know, I've known plenty of cadets like you,"
interrupted Boothby. He shook his head as he bent down
and stuck his dirty spade into the rich topsoil.

"That's nice, sir," she said, wondering how she was
going to make it back to the dorm in record time. "But
really, I have to—"

"One cadet in particular. His name was Paraday."

She hesitated. "You mean Admiral Paraday? Of the
Orion Expedition?" she asked, dropping two data padds
in the process. She stared at the padds, but didn't move.

"Same."

"He's . . . well, he's a legend. Everyone knows about him."

"That's right, and like you and every other cadet, he started here at Starfleet Academy," Boothby said, resuming his digging. "Yes, he was impatient like you. Always in a hurry. Not focusing on anything. Bold. Brassy. Always wanting to get ahead faster than anyone would let him. But his impatience was causing him to fail. To be nervous and fumbling. So he invented something to focus on. He called it Paraday's Ladder."

"Paraday's Ladder? What's that?"

"A vision he kept of a ladder. His own ladder. And each day, he'd step up one more step. One step at a time. No hurry—just at the right pace."

"Where did the ladder go?" asked Kathryn, hoping to stump the groundskeeper.

"To the stars, Cadet," said Boothby, his face turning slightly to look up to the bright sunlit sky. "To the stars."

Kathryn took a deep breath and let it out slowly. She reached down and picked up the padds, carefully stacking them in her left arm again. "Paraday's Ladder? I like it. Thanks, Mr. Boothby."

"Boothby."

"Huh?"

"Just Boothby, Cadet."

"Yes, sir . . . I mean, Boothby. My name is Kathryn Janeway."

"I know," Boothby said, winking at Kathryn. "Have

fun on the *Tsiolkovsky*," he added, whistling as he continued to dig a hole for a nearby rosebush.

Kathryn stared at the groundskeeper for a second, then walked carefully around the flowers to her dorm. First Geordi knew about the cadets on the *Tsiolkovsky*, and now Boothby.

Some secret, she thought.

Chapter

2

Kathryn pushed her bag strap up on her shoulder for what seemed like the hundredth time. She was on her way to meet with the other *Tsiolkovsky* cadets to catch the shuttle to Paris, and she had two minutes left to reach the platform.

It wasn't her fault. It just seemed as if everything were against her. First, she couldn't find her antigrav boots, standard equipment for every cadet when packing for off-world travel. Next, it took time to find the basalt rock she always kept with her—the one her father found when they once hiked the canyons of Mars. Then the communication link between Starfleet Academy and her parents on Mars was slow, the result of a stronger-than-usual solar storm. And to top everything off, her mother and sister, Phoebe, were the only ones there. Her father was at an important Federation meeting.

Kathryn ran past a group of cadets reading a wall monitor. Her eye caught the title of the announcement: *Tsiolkovsky* Mission Cadets. "Hey, Kathryn," one of the cadets yelled as she scurried by. "Congratulations! Send me a telepostcard!"

She suddenly swelled with pride. Finally, after the first few months of constant struggle, she felt as if she were really getting somewhere at Starfleet Academy. She pulled on the bag and yelled back, "You bet."

As Kathryn rounded the corner of the shuttle building, she gasped. The shuttle doors were beginning to close—the engines ready for takeoff!

She ran at top speed to the platform, but the doors hissed shut before she could make it inside. Desperate, she started to bang on the door, hoping that somehow, it would open again. Looking through the window, she saw L'as'wa Ranna run over and push a panel on the wall. Kathryn practically fell through the door as it whisked open.

"Kathron!" exclaimed L'as'wa, half catching Kathryn in her arms. "I was beginning to worry."

"*You* were beginning to worry?" she answered, giving her friend a relieved look.

L'as'wa was a Hassic, and like all her people, she was beautiful, with dark, round eyes and light-colored skin. She was studying to become a starship navigator, and Kathryn knew she was one of the top cadets in math at the Academy. Kathryn also noticed—besides the fact that all the cadets seemed to stare when L'as'wa walked by—that the Hassic's medium-length blond hair was always straight and perfect, a look that Kathryn could never seem to achieve. It was the only thing that drove her crazy about L'as'wa. But *anyone* whose hair was nicer than hers drove Kathryn crazy—*and that,* she thought, *included just about everyone in the universe.*

"What happened, Kathron?" L'as'wa's Hassic accent made it difficult to pronounce Kathryn's name.

"It was a wild morning," she answered, dropping her gear in an empty seat. "You wouldn't believe—"

"Wild morning or not, a cadet learns . . . sss to be on time," hissed a raspy voice behind her, grating on her already fragile nerves. Kathryn turned to face Blinar, who was looking down his long, bumpy nose at her. The cadet's brown and white mottled, feathery ears were wiggling quickly back and forth—which Kathryn knew was a sign of aggression. Blinar was from Tegi, a planet within the Federation and Romulan Neutral Zone. She knew his people were confrontational, and she could understand why. For about a century, they had been fighting off Romulan raids on their homeworld. But she didn't want a confrontation—not today, of all days. She gritted her teeth to keep from arguing.

"Blinar. She was exactly on time," said L'as'wa, stepping between the two cadets. "She is here. Is she not?" she asked in her usual clipped sentences.

Blinar's scaled face scowled at L'as'wa, his ears quivering slightly. "Then my *suggestion* is . . . sss that she arrive a little before the assigned time," he said, deliberately ignoring Kathryn, "so she can at least approach the

shuttle calmly—not beat down the door." He turned and headed for a seat in the front of the shuttle.

L'as'wa shrugged at Kathryn and sat down. "I have noticed. Every day is a bad day. Especially for him."

"Right. But just once I'd like to tell him—"

"Kathron. It is not worth it," she interrupted, carefully pronouncing each syllable.

Kathryn dropped into the seat next to L'as'wa. "All right. Just this time, though. He's not in charge—even if his reporting officer *is* the captain of the *Tsiolkovsky.*"

As the student pilot slipped the shuttle out of its port, the students buckled their safety harnesses. Kathryn looked around. The other two chosen cadets, Mari Lakoo and Timothy Yang, sat in the rear seats, intently discussing the information they were reading on a data padd. Both cadets were short and dark haired, and Kathryn knew in the short time they had attended the Academy, they had become best friends. Mari was from northern North America, and was a descendent of the Yupiaq, an ancient Eskimo culture. Timothy was from San Francisco, not far from Starfleet Headquarters. He once told Kathryn that his great-great-grandfather was one of the people who helped form the United Federation of Planets in 2161. It seemed as if all of his relatives since then were in Starfleet in one capacity or another.

Kathryn reached in her bag for a data padd. She still had twenty minutes before the shuttle reached Paris. She might as well go over her notes about the mission. As she turned on the small padd, she yawned, then closed her eyes. "I could sure go for one of my mother's caramel brownies about now," she muttered to no one in particular.

After the shuttle reached Paris, events happened at an astounding rate. And before she knew it, Kathryn was standing at attention in front of Captain Gary Wingate onboard the *Tsiolkovsky.* "Welcome to the *U.S.S. Tsiolkovsky,*" announced the captain, staring at the five cadets.

Kathryn looked straight ahead, hoping the captain didn't notice the beads of sweat forming on her forehead. She had seen Captain Wingate's file before coming onboard, and she knew he was one of the youngest captains in Starfleet—and one of the best. Kathryn noted that in person, the captain was much more imposing than the holoimage in his file. He was just over six feet tall, with brown eyes and brown hair, and stood as if he had been in command from the time he was born. *I wonder how he does that,* she thought.

"We are now heading for the planet Chatoob," Captain Wingate continued. "You may want to know, Cadet Ranna, that we are on a heading of 033, Mark 15." He nodded to the Hassic cadet, then continued. "As you all know, you have been assigned to this starship to help us on this humanitarian mission. Besides dropping off medical equipment, we may be doing some preliminary negotiations to see if the Chatoob wish to join the Federation." He looked at each cadet in turn. "I must emphasize that you are all representatives of Starfleet and you will act accordingly. I hope you will learn a great deal from your experiences here and from your assigned bridge officers. Any questions?" When no one responded, the captain put his hands on his hips and nodded to the exit. "Now go stow your gear in your assigned quarters. Then meet with the first officer, Commander Pago-Pago, in Transporter Room Two. You have work to do."

And that's when the "fun" began.

Kathryn and the others scurried to their rooms and back to Transporter Room Two. Commander Pago-Pago was already there, and as the cadets lined up near the transporter console, he instructed the transporter chief to energize. Numerous containers and packages of all sizes and colors materialized on the pads. The commander then told the cadets to grab the boxes and take them to the offices on the labels. The cadets dispersed, carrying as many packages as they could in their arms.

As the door of the transporter room whisked open, Kathryn heard Blinar muttering under his breath—about how they were not being treated like cadets, but like delivery people. Deep down inside, Kathryn agreed, but she said nothing.

An hour later, she was beginning to feel as if she had run several miles. Her feet and legs hurt, and her arms didn't feel much better. As she leaned against a bulkhead on Deck Twelve, her badge chimed and she was called to Transporter Room Four. "Oh, no, not more packages," she moaned, pushing herself from the wall. "I know, I know. One step at a time, Kathryn," she recited and practically ran to the turbolift.

The other cadets were already there when she arrived. Commander Pago-Pago was explaining their next assignment: Take an inventory of the weapons inside the transporter room.

Then came the inch-by-inch demagnetization of the transporter, with Kathryn and the other cadets scanning the pads on their knees.

And finally, the commander took the cadets to a broken hallway computer panel on Deck Ten. Kathryn was amazed at how they all sorted through the problem, and together found a way to fix the broken panel. Even Blinar was cooperating, his ears hardly moving as he worked. *Maybe he's too tired to be obnoxious,* she thought. *I know I am.*

At the end of the day, Captain Wingate stood before the exhausted cadets, beaming broadly. "And you thought all we did was sit on the bridge," he said, jokingly. Kathryn noticed Timothy tried to smile, but it looked more like a grimace. "Cadets dismissed."

The next morning, Kathryn, half-asleep, looked around the galley and wondered how she got there, or even how she managed to put on her starship uniform. Ignoring the thought, she grabbed a steaming cup of coffee from the replicator and dropped down into a chair. She closed her eyes and sniffed deeply. "Bring me back to life, please," she muttered to the coffee cup.

"Are you talking to me, Kathron?" asked Kathryn's starship roommate L'as'wa, slipping into the seat across from Kathryn. Timothy, Mari, and Blinar also sat down, setting their breakfast trays on the table.

"No, I'm talking to this coffee cup," she said, not opening her eyes.

"I see. It does not surprise me, Kathron. Talking to coffee cups," L'as'wa said, chuckling. Kathryn lifted an eyelid to look at her roommate. To her dismay, she noticed that the Hassic's blond hair was perfect and didn't even move as she laughed. She closed her eye again.

"I always talk to coffee cups, don't you, Mari?" asked Timothy, chewing a piece of toast.

"I make it a daily habit," his friend responded cheerfully.

Kathryn opened her eyes slowly and stared at the two friends. "Why aren't you two exhausted?" she asked.

"Where food is concerned, they're always . . . sss happy," said Blinar, digging into a green and brown concoction on his plate—no doubt a Tegi delicacy.

"That's right. Mari and I have eaten our way through some of the best restaurants in San Francisco. We're thinking of writing restaurant reviews for the Academy newspaper," said Timothy. He leaned over the table and looked at Blinar's plate. "What's that, Blinar?"

"Tegi toad fish," he answered, his mottled ears moving slightly.

Kathryn chuckled as Mari and Timothy leaned back in their chairs, each making a face. "So much for the great gourmets of Starfleet Academy." She turned to her roommate. "Aren't you eating this morning, L'as'wa?"

"My people eat small meals," she answered in her usual short sentences. "We eat several times a day. This is not one of the times. I will go to our quarters for a while. I want to work on the Planetary Exploration paper. Lieutenant Muldov's course is most difficult."

"And he tried to assign us extra homework at a time like this," added Kathryn, trying but failing to push a stray lock of hair from her face. "Luckily, he cut back the homework when he found out we were going on this mission."

A small smile crossed L'as'wa's lips. She leaned across the table toward Kathryn and lowered her voice. "I fooled him. I said we were gone for four days. Not seven. Too much homework would cause my second stomach to be eaten away by excess acid."

"*You're* the reason why we have less . . . sss homework?" hissed Blinar, squinting as he looked down his nose at L'as'wa. The Hassic nodded, smiling triumphantly.

"Sneak," whispered Kathryn, smiling back. "But an ingenious sneak."

Mari wiped his mouth with a napkin. "Good job, L'as'wa. But how did your stomachs do yesterday?" he asked, then turned to the others. "Do you believe what we did—and all in one afternoon?"

"I thought we would take our stations on arrival," L'as'wa said. "We would be with officers on the bridge. I had no idea. Cleanup and delivery duty all over the ship." L'as'wa sighed and threw a strand of hair back over her shoulder. Kathryn noticed it fell right into place. "I will see you later, Cadets."

As L'as'wa stood up and walked out the galley door, Kathryn shook her head. She could sympathize with her Hassic roommate. They all had hoped to meet their assigned bridge officers immediately upon arrival, and L'as'wa had her hopes set on learning all she could from the bridge navigator. Kathryn herself had yet to meet

Emma Tapper, one of the most well-known science officers in Starfleet.

She closed her eyes again and took a sip of coffee.

"I always thought it had something to do with the ocean." A woman's voice behind Kathryn caught her attention.

"What do you mean 'ocean'?" came the mocking answer, the man's voice booming and echoing off the galley's walls. Kathryn's eyes popped open. "A planet's atmospheric color isn't something that's controlled by the colors of the ocean. What if a planet doesn't have an ocean? No, it's something else, but I'll be hanged if I know."

Kathryn looked at Timothy, who shrugged. Then she turned around in her seat and faced a man and a woman in Starfleet Medical blue at a nearby table.

"Ummm . . . excuse us . . . I think we can help," she said, hesitating as the two officers stared at the cadets.

"It's really a simple concept," said Mari, pushing his plate out of the way.

"Yes," added Kathryn. "The reason why a planet's atmosphere is a certain color is because of the way starlight is scattered by molecules in the planet's atmosphere. In Earth's atmosphere, the longer wavelengths pass through, but the shorter blue rays are scattered in all directions, giving it a blue hue."

"Mine is a mostly water planet," responded Blinar proudly, "and our atmosphere looks . . . sss blue from space, too."

"And did you know that several centuries ago on Earth, spacecraft images from the solar system's planets were falsely enhanced," added Timothy, getting into the explanation. "They thought some of the planets were certain colors, when in reality, they were more bland colors."

No one said a word. Kathryn hesitated as they continued to stare at the cadets. "Does . . . does that make sense?"

"You're the cadets traveling with us, aren't you?" said the man, almost as if he ignored their explanation.

For a second, Kathryn shrank back from the booming voice, then straightened her shoulders. "Yes, sir. I'm Cadet Kathryn Janeway, sir. And these are cadets Blinar, Mari Lakoo, and Timothy Wang." The others nodded in the doctors' direction.

"Yes, I can tell you're Academy all right," he said, almost accusingly. "Well, thanks for your explanations, but I already have entirely too much information crammed into my brain about people problems without worrying about a planet's atmosphere, thank you." He stood up, his tall, thick frame dwarfing the chair he was sitting in. "Doctor. Cadets," he said gruffly. He walked out the galley door, his head barely missing the top of the door frame.

"I'm sorry, Cadets. I'm Dr. Sara Hess," said the thin woman at the table, motioning for the others to sit down opposite her. She pushed back a lock of short red hair from her forehead. "I must apologize for my colleague. Dr. Bennia Tobassa is a bit ornery in the morning— especially if you ask him to think."

"That's okay," said Kathryn, shrugging. "My sister, Phoebe, is the same way in the morning. She loves to stay up late, then wonders why she's so tired and grouchy in the morning. And of course, she *never* listens to me when I try to explain it."

Dr. Hess laughed. "Well, Cadets, anytime you want to come down to sickbay and give me an explanation of planetary atmospheres, please do. I won't be grumpy about it." She looked down as her comm badge chirped.

"Sickbay to Hess."

"Hess here, go ahead, Doctor," she answered. Kathryn recognized the booming voice.

"Tobassa here. They've managed to isolate that rotten biofilter. Want to check it out?"

"I'll be right there." Dr. Hess touched her comm badge. "Remember, Cadets, my door is always open." Kathryn and the others nodded as the doctor turned to leave.

I think I'm going to like this place, Kathryn thought, heading to the replicator for another cup of coffee.

Chapter

3

Chatoob was only a few hundred thousand kilometers away when the *Tsiolkovsky* came out of warp. Kathryn was fully awake now and finally standing next to Science Officer Lieutenant Commander Emma Tapper at the bridge's Science Station. Kathryn could see almost everything from the aft section of the bridge when she turned from her science monitor, including the large viewscreen that covered almost a third of the far bridge wall. She had a hard time ignoring the viewscreen. It was the first time she had ever seen stars when a ship was in warp drive, the elongated shapes cut by a spectrum of color.

Dragging her eyes from the viewscreen, she noted the other cadets standing next to their assigned officers: L'as'wa Ranna was standing next to the navigator's station, Mari Lakoo was next to the helm, and Blinar was to the right of Captain Wingate's chair. Only Timothy Wang was missing, assigned to the engineering room several decks down.

"Impulse power, Mr. Wright," ordered the captain to the helmsman.

As Mari watched, Lieutenant Wright pressed several templates. "Aye, sir," Wright responded. "Planet in visual range, sir."

"Magnify." Lieutenant Wright leaned back and allowed Mari to enter the magnification codes.

Kathryn couldn't help it. She was staring at the viewscreen again. The planet's surface suddenly filled the entire screen. There were numerous deep blue oceans and small seas. Two large landmasses—mixes of yellows and browns, with patches of green—were on this side of the planet. Kathryn also spotted a tiny moon traveling across the face of Chatoob, cutting between the ship and the planet.

But even more striking were the domes that covered parts of the upper continent, looking like huge lumps on the skin of the planet's surface. Kathryn was amazed by the domes' structural design—a crisscrossing of tall metal beams and thick crystal posts. The outside of the domes seemed to be covered with diamonds, sparkling from the reflection of Chatoob's sun. Kathryn suddenly realized that solar cell panels probably created the effect, as they collected the much needed energy from the nearest star.

"ETA ten minutes to orbit, sir," said Wright, breaking the silence.

"Ten minutes?" responded the captain. He spun in his

chair and turned to Blinar. "And what do we know about this planet, Mr. Blinar?"

Kathryn rolled her eyes as Blinar stood ramrod straight in front of the captain. *He just seems to try too hard,* she thought, looking back at her monitor.

"Sir," Blinar began. "We know that Chatoob is . . . sss an M-class planet. We know that the first brief, long-distance contact with the planet's people was made at least ten years ago by the Klingons . . . sss," he recited, his raspy voice making Kathryn uneasy. "They claimed the Chatoob were on the verge of solar system exploration. It is a domed society and the Chatoob government indicated that the planet's air had not been fit to breathe for about one standard Earth-century, polluted with chemicals . . . sss and bacteria by industrial groups—and they claim it was . . . sss the fault of the old government." He paused and took a deep breath before continuing. "The Chatoob people are humanoid, all with white hair, light olive skin, flat ears, three fingers . . . sss, and their large eyes can see visible and a small amount of infrared light . . . sir."

Captain Wingate smiled at the Tegi. "Very impressive, Mr. Blinar. But you forgot one thing: Chatoob has two major cultures—the Chat and the Obers. The Chats run the government at the moment."

Blinar's ears wiggled slightly. "I didn't think that was . . . sss important, sir."

Captain Wingate was still smiling. "Every piece of information is important, Cadet. Even if it seems trivial to you at the moment."

Kathryn was half listening to the conversation. Right

now, she was intent on the readings coming from the planet. She ran a sensor scan, then tried it again. It gave her the same answer. Something was wrong here— maybe something with the sensors? "Lieutenant Tapper?"

"Yes, Cadet Janeway," answered the science officer, turning from listening to the exchange between the captain and Blinar.

"Would you please check me on this?" Kathryn's hands were starting to sweat.

Captain Wingate turned in the direction of the Science Station. "Something wrong, Cadet Janeway?"

"Sir, I don't understand it," she said, hesitating. She looked from Lieutenant Tapper to the captain, then took a deep breath. "According to the readings, the air on the planet is breathable by human standards." The science officer nodded in confirmation.

"Explanation?" the captain asked.

"I don't know, sir," Kathryn said. She turned to the science officer, then back to the monitor. "A-according to the sensors," Kathryn continued, "there was an apparent problem with the air maybe a half century ago— chemicals, bacteria, and such—but not much anymore. In fact, the domes seem to have more pollutants inside than they do outside." She looked up at the captain. "And, sir, the domes are apparently connected by underground tunnels, and *they* have even more pollutants than the outside." Lieutenant Tapper nodded in agreement at the captain.

"Then why do they still insist on living in the domes?" Captain Wingate said, almost to himself. "All right.

Janeway. Tapper. I want answers. See if the people on the planet can't stand something in the atmosphere that humans can—and that's why they're still living in the domes. Or see if there is some type of natural hazard out there that might harm the population. I want all the possibilities explored."

"Aye, sir." Kathryn's fingers flew over the panel's templates as Science Officer Tapper looked over her left shoulder. Suddenly, Kathryn noticed someone was standing on her right.

It was Blinar.

"Let me know if you need help, Lieutenant Commander Tapper," he said smugly, looking down his bumpy nose at the officer. "I did quite well on the sensor analysis . . . sss tests to enter the Academy. And as the captain will tell you, it's best for a captain to know all the systems on his bridge."

Janeway bit her lip in anger and tried to concentrate on her task. She knew what she was doing. She didn't need Blinar pushing his way into her work—especially something this important.

"I think you're running under a misconception, Mr. Blinar," said the science officer, folding her arms across her chest. "A captain allows his crew to do their work as a well-functioning team, Mr. Blinar. And Cadet Janeway is doing her job very well."

Blinar scowled, his ears twitching once. "Yes . . . sss. Good point." He turned slowly and walked back to stand next to the captain.

Kathryn looked at Lieutenant Tapper and smiled. "Thanks for the support."

"You deserve it," she said, leaning over to get closer to the monitor. "Now I just can't see why they insist on living in those domes. Why would they report such bad contamination conditions?"

Kathryn noticed the green glow from the environmental readings remained steady as she scanned the entire planet—meaning there were few pollutants in the air. "I have no idea," she said, shaking her head. "Maybe their sensors aren't as good as ours. But don't worry. I'll figure it out while I'm down on the planet."

The science officer raised an eyebrow and laughed. "And what makes you think you're going on the away team?" she asked.

"Commander Pago-Pago," said the captain, suddenly turning to his first officer. "I want you, Doctors Hess and Tobassa—and all five of the cadets—on the away team. We'll contact the Chats and tell them you'll soon be on your way."

It was Kathryn's turn to raise an eyebrow. She smiled at a surprised Lieutenant Commander Tapper and headed for the turbolift.

"Tobassa do this, Tobassa do that. I joined Starfleet to treat people, not carry packages to other planets." Dr. Bennia Tobassa grabbed another small box in his huge hands and carried it to the transporter pad.

"They're not just packages, Bennia," answered Dr. Hess. "It's medical equipment. And we're trying to help these people, remember?"

"Right, right. But just for once, can't we send down something that doesn't weigh at least two hundred pounds? Why not just send down a bunch of medical tricorders? That would be enough to keep them going for a while."

Kathryn carried another box to the transporter platform and smiled. For ten minutes, she and the other cadets stacked boxes for transport and listened to Drs. Hess and Tobassa toss comments back and forth. Apparently, it didn't matter what time of the day it was. Kathryn noticed that Dr. Tobassa just loved to complain.

"It doesn't weigh two hundred pounds, Bennia," Dr. Hess countered. She looked over at the cadets helping to load the cargo on the transporter pads. "And you're giving these young cadets the wrong idea about what it's like to be a doctor in Starfleet Medical."

"Are any of you going to be a doctor?" Dr. Tobassa asked, his loud voice echoing around the transporter room. All the cadets shook their heads. "There you go, Sara. These cadets don't want to deliver medical equipment. They want to become starship captains, right?" Without waiting for an answer, he continued, "You don't see the captain down here loading equipment, do you?"

Dr. Hess shook her head at Kathryn and wiped her forehead with her shirtsleeve. "Don't listen to him. He just came back from a wonderfully relaxing vacation in Earth's Antarctica—you know, the penguin rookery. Then he had to go on this mission, so he's a bit cranky." Kathryn smiled, realizing that all Dr. Hess seemed to do was make excuses for her colleague. "All right, Cadets. I think we're ready. Hess to bridge."

"Bridge here," came the captain's crisp reply.

"Ready to transport, Captain. Seventy pounds of

equipment," she said, pointedly looking at Dr. Tobassa, "along with two doctors, and five cadets—ready to go."

"Good," he replied. "Commander Pago-Pago and two security officers will follow you down directly."

Kathryn stood on the transporter platform and checked to make sure she had her comm badge and science tricorder. As Dr. Hess gave the order to energize, Kathryn closed her eyes. It was a habit she picked up years ago, when she first transported with her father to Starfleet Headquarters in San Francisco from her home in Indiana. Even though she had heard how safe and easy it was to be transported, she still was scared. But she wouldn't let her father know. So she closed her eyes, thought about her favorite climbing tree, and before she knew what was happening, she was on the far side of the continent. This time, too, she closed her eyes—and opened them to see six tall humanoids bowing in front of her.

The tallest of the group held up his right hand, his three long, thin fingers outstretched in a sign of greeting. "Welcome to Chatoob," he said, his sharp, deep voice speaking so fast that Kathryn had a hard time understanding him. His hair seemed to move, as if he were in a breeze. "I am Govenoral Nema. I and my officials welcome you to our government headquarters."

Kathryn watched as Dr. Hess returned his gesture and nodded slightly. Commander Pago-Pago and two security officers materialized, and the commander, too, saluted the govenoral with the Chatoob greeting.

As the commander introduced his away team, Kathryn tried to stand at attention and look straight ahead. But out of the corner of her eye, she studied the Chatoob people. Just as her mission profile mentioned, the Chatoob had vivid white hair and large sky blue eyes. The two females wore their hair in long braids; while the men's hair stood up straight and spiked. Six small, round metal dots circled their flat ears. The three fingers on each hand were long and thin, decorated with rings of many colors. All of the officials were dressed in extremely neat, crisp uniforms: rich-looking dark blue jackets, trimmed across the chest in braids of red and green and what looked like real gold. The pants were also lined along the sides with gold, ending with a round medallion. Just below the jacket cuff on the left wrist, the officials wore what looked like a small rose, each a different color.

"And these are the Starfleet Academy cadets Captain Wingate mentioned," the commander was saying, introducing each of the cadets in turn.

"Ah, Cadets," Govenoral Nema said quickly, turning to the cadets. He raised his nose and seemed to sniff the air, his spikes of hair waving. "I am pleased you are here to witness the joint cooperation between our two peoples." He looked at Kathryn. "And I see you are interested in our attire, Cadet, especially our wrist-watchers." One long finger pointed to his wrist and he sniffed again toward Kathryn. "What was your name again?"

"Janeway, sir. Cadet Kathryn Janeway," she said, trying hard to keep up with his rapid speech. She found herself talking almost as fast as the Chatoob leader.

"Kathryn? We have a word that is similar in our language. It means 'seeker.' " He pulled at his jacket sleeve, revealing his left wrist. "And the wrist-watchers, you may ask? They tell us whether or not there are any leaks of noxious gases from outside of the domes seeping into our world. They are called Tana flowers, of the Hether-oob family, and are quite profuse. Everyone in the dome wears one all of the time. And if they wither in any way, it is an indication that gases are present." Govenoral Nema seemed to shudder, his hair waving more rapidly, almost in time with his voice.

"Sounds familiar," said Pago-Pago, standing closer to the govenoral to look at the wrist-watcher. "We used to extract mineral and metal resources from mines deep in the earth centuries ago on our planet. They used a certain bird called a canary to detect if there were any bad gases in the mine. If the canary died, it was a good bet that the air wasn't fit for humans, either."

Kathryn shifted slightly as everyone waited for Govenoral Nema's response. He sniffed at the air, said nothing, and turned his attention to the cadets again. "You are all welcome here. And, if you don't mind, we would like you to wear the wrist-watchers during your stay." He watched as each person in the *Tsiolkovsky* group was given a Tana flower. The govenoral suddenly frowned, his large forehead wrinkling over his wide eyes. "But I must warn you: Do not explore the outside of this complex and do not talk to anyone outside of my officials. Although my people know you are here, they are very cautious around visitors. And of course, do not wander outside of the dome."

As Kathryn took the bright yellow Tana flower

handed to her by one of the officials, she glanced at the first officer. *That's great,* she thought, *now I'll never figure out what's wrong with the air outside the dome. There goes my chance to impress the captain and Emma Tapper.*

The morning went slowly. Mari, Timothy, and Blinar unloaded each box; Kathryn and L'as'wa noted its contents and checked it off on their data padds. Drs. Hess and Tobassa would then instruct the Chatoob officials how to use the instrument. But it was a long process. The Chatoob often wanted something explained at least four or five times and Kathryn wondered if they couldn't understand the doctors' *slower* speech. She admired Dr. Hess's patience not only in dealing with the Chatoob, but with the complaining Dr. Tobassa.

"I think that's the end of the heater packs," said Kathryn, showing her data padd to Dr. Hess. "Commander Pago-Pago just beamed up to the *Tsiolkovsky* to check on the last boxes to be transported."

Dr. Hess nodded and looked over Kathryn's shoulder at the data padd. "Looks like we're doing fine." She looked around the large room. "Did you notice the crystals in the windows around here, Kathryn?"

Kathryn nodded and pointed directly overhead. "That one is beautiful, especially when the artificial sunlight from the dome generator hits it just right. Do you think the crystals are natural?"

"You're the scientist," Dr. Hess said, chuckling. "You tell me."

Kathryn pulled out her tricorder and began scanning,

spinning around to take in the entire crystal. "That's strange—"

"Hess!" came a booming voice. "The commander just checked in. Only two more boxes coming our way. Let's hurry up. This wrist-watcher is making me itch," he said, moving the flower farther up his arm and out of the way.

Dr. Hess nodded to Dr. Tobassa, then turned back to Kathryn. "Is something wrong?"

"No, not really. I just had a weird reading. Now it's gone."

Dr. Hess hesitated, then leaned closer to Kathryn. "Listen. You told me earlier you wanted to find out more about the air outside the dome. So why don't you look around? Check out the crystals and take some tricorder readings. I know this complex isn't far from the outside of the dome."

Kathryn brightened. *Then I can find out what's going on around here,* she thought. "That sounds like a great idea, Dr. Hess," she said out loud.

"I'm sure we can handle the rest, right, Bennia?"

"Sure. What's a few more hundred pounds of boxes?"

As Dr. Hess frowned in mock anger at her colleague, Kathryn walked over to L'as'wa. "Time for a break," she said, then turned to the other cadets. "Let's take a look at this building."

"Kathryn," said Timothy, bowing in her direction. "My muscles thank you."

"Don't get swellheaded, Kathryn," responded Mari. "He has no muscles."

As the five cadets walked down a nearby corridor, Kathryn was amazed how the walls seemed to shift in a prism effect as light struck the crystals. Timothy ran his hand along the sleek, colorful wall. "It almost looks as if this wall—and every other wall and ceiling around here—is made entirely of crystal. It's like a crystal palace."

Kathryn nodded and ran her tricorder up and down the sides of the hallway. "It's some kind of quartzlike crystal, but it's almost flawless. I had no idea the Chatoob people had such skills. I wonder if they grow these crystals to be this large?"

"Maybe they mined them?" asked Mari.

"Maybe," answered Kathryn, "but on Earth, quartz crystals don't grow this large, and if they did, they would have too many flaws in them, like bubbles and pieces of organics."

"So they have to be manufactured. Right?" asked L'as'wa, touching the wall gently with the tip of her index finger.

Blinar suddenly sighed, walking in front of the group. "Manufactured. Mined. Or from eggs . . . sss laid by Lojellian starfish!" he said, his ears moving back and forth in frustration. "Who cares how this . . . sss rock was made?"

Timothy stood in front of Blinar, squinting his eyes. "Well, maybe some of us are interested in the world around them. Maybe some of us aren't trying to act like they know everything all the time."

"Oh, yeah?"

"Yeah."

"Well, I s . . . sssuppose you think that I—"

"Wait a minute!" Kathryn interrupted, ignoring the

two cadets and turning in a small circle. "Quiet for a minute. There's something here . . ." She tapped a tricorder template twice. "There," she said, pointing toward the end of the hallway. "That reading again. It's in that direction."

Kathryn walked ahead of the others, moving down the long corridor and stopping at the end. To the left was a dead end; to the right was a short hallway with a large windowed door at the end. Her tricorder began to hum again, and as she looked into the window, Kathryn gasped. Standing there was a shawled, bent-over old female Chatoob, her three wrinkled fingers grasping the handle of a dark-colored cane.

Kathryn turned to the others. "Over here!" she yelled. And as she turned back to the window, the old woman was gone!

Surprised, she shook her head. Was she just imagining it? And if she wasn't, why would such a ragged looking person be in the government building—especially when everyone else in the complex was dressed so neatly. And why did she keep getting such strange readings on her tricorder—especially when she pointed the instrument in the old woman's direction?

Looking back, she saw the others arguing and realized they hadn't heard her yell. Kathryn easily made up her mind: It was better to check this herself than try to attract the cadets' attention. Kathryn knew it would just take too long. *And anyway,* she thought, *maybe this door leads to doors to the outside of the dome.*

Holding her tricorder in front of her, she moved cautiously down the short hallway to the door. The strange emissions were completely gone now, disappearing like the old woman.

She put her hand on the doorknob just as someone placed a hand on her shoulder!

"Kathron. What are you doing?"

Kathryn jumped. "L'as'wa!" she exclaimed. "Don't ever do that."

"We did not see you all of the sudden," she said, then pointed to the others standing behind her. "We thought you disappeared."

"No, but someone else did," she said, explaining to the others about the old woman and the strange readings on her tricorder. "I was just going to see where she went," she added, turning the doorknob.

The door swung open slowly. Kathryn was in the lead, with the four cadets following close behind. For some reason, Kathryn and the others tiptoed in the room, almost as if they were entering the Academy library. There was another small hallway, and another door—this time with a smaller crystal window. Again, Kathryn turned the doorknob and the cadets stepped through the opened door, entering a small room no bigger than her dorm room.

Fixtures along the ceiling bathed the room in a bright yellow light. "I wonder what this room is for," asked Mari, squinting his eyes. "These lights look like the ones that simulate sunlight in the greenhouses and hydrochambers."

"Where are the plants?" asked L'as'wa, almost in a whisper.

"I don't know," answered Blinar firmly, his ears going

flat against his head. "But I think we should go back and help Dr. Hess unload the rest of the boxes . . . sss. Not go on some wild duck chase."

"That's goose chase," replied Timothy, rolling his eyes.

"Well, *I* just want to find out if I'm going crazy," explained Kathryn, shading her eyes and looking around the empty room. "Plus, if I can learn anything about the air outside the domes, I'd—"

Before Kathryn finished her sentence, the door they entered slammed shut. Just as suddenly, alarms started chiming and ringing. She dropped her tricorder and covered her ears to shut out the noise. The instrument bounced across the room. As Kathryn watched in dismay, a thick metal plate slid over the exit—crushing the tricorder under its weight!

They all covered their ears but it was no use. The ringing was so loud, it was painful. Kathryn saw L'as'wa's lips moving, but it was impossible to hear her.

Then suddenly, the lights went out.

And even though the alarms still blared, Kathryn was sure she heard Mari's voice.

"We're trapped!"

Chapter

4

Kathryn reached her arms forward, trying to forget that her ears hurt from the noise. Feeling the cool wall, she worked her way back toward the direction of the door they had entered. Suddenly, her fingers came in contact with a thick, hard seam, and she knew she had reached the sealed door.

Ignoring the painful noise, she tried to move the metal seal by wedging her fingers in the seam and pulling hard. "Ouch," she yelled, but the ringing was still so loud she couldn't hear her own voice. The metal cover wouldn't budge.

As the Klaxons continued to blare, Kathryn thought she heard someone trying to yell above the noise. "And if we just . . . maybe if you . . . can everyone hear me?"

It was Blinar trying to yell orders to the others—but to no avail.

Suddenly, the alarms stopped.

Kathryn felt her ears ringing. She shook her head, but the ringing continued.

"Hey! Can anyone hear us?" yelled Timothy. He turned to L'as'wa. "You have a loud voice. Start yelling."

L'as'wa looked hurt and confused for a second, then realized it might help. "Is anyone out there? Can you hear us?" she started yelling, her voice bouncing off the walls of the small room. Kathryn held her ears again.

"Wait," said Blinar, holding up his hand, his ears twitching quickly. "Do you hear s . . . sssomething?"

"Just my ears ringing louder than a town filled with church bells," replied Mari. Suddenly, he tilted his head, listening. And as he did, Kathryn took her hands from her ears and listened, too.

There was a slow ticking noise, as if someone were tapping on the wall. The tapping became louder and faster. Noise started to fill the room again, but it was the sound of gears creaking and grinding slowly. As the noises became louder and louder, Kathryn caught a movement out of the corner of her eye.

"Circle—pattern Delta!" Blinar yelled. It was the best way to protect each other and to see what was going on. The five cadets rapidly formed a circle, their backs to each other. As they watched, two of the solid walls began to rise revealing huge crystal windows on opposite sides of the room.

Through the window opposite Kathryn was Govenoral

Nema and several of his officers, all standing at attention, and with looks of disgust on their long faces.

Kathryn heard L'as'wa gasp loudly behind her. Turning, she saw what made her Hassic roommate cry out. The second wall-window on the other side of the room revealed a grim sight: Dozens of bedraggled Chatoobs—many in makeshift beds—staring at the cadets through the window. Kathryn thought she saw the old woman, but she couldn't make out the figure in the dimly lit room.

"I am shocked, Federation Cadets," said Govenoral Nema, his severe voice resounding over a loudspeaker in the small, sealed room. He sighed heavily, his spiked hair beginning to wave as he sniffed the air, then continued in his rapid speech. "You were told not to wander outside of our complex. We thought your people had a bit more sense than to go against the laws of our people."

"I'll handle this . . . sss," Blinar whispered to the others, and stepped forward. "Govenoral Nema," he said loudly, "we broke no laws. And we did not wander outs . . . ssside of the complex."

"We have witnesses that you—"

"Govenoral, we were only meters . . . sss away from where we trans . . . sssported down," Blinar interrupted, his hissing becoming more pronounced.

"—we have witnesses," Nema said, talking over Blinar, his words almost running together as he yelled over the communications panel, "that you were outside the complex!"

Blinar's ears twitched madly as he started to lunge

toward the huge window. L'as'wa put her hand on his shoulder. "No, Blinar. What are you going to do? Crash through the window?"

Kathryn nodded in agreement and said, "Let's hear what he has to say."

Govenoral Nema leaned toward one of his officers and whispered in his ear. The official nodded, sniffed once, and whispered back. "It is unfortunate," the govenoral said, clearing his throat, "that you did not listen to our instructions. My assistant now informs me that you have all been exposed to a deadly disease—one that is a grave threat to many of our people. We wiped it out once, but it is now back."

"What? That's abs . . . sssurd!" said Blinar, moving again toward the window. This time, Kathryn and L'as'wa held him back.

Timothy slapped his chest to activate his communicator. "Cadet Wang to *Tsiolkovsky*. Come in, bridge . . . Cadet Wang to—"

Govenoral Nema cleared his throat again and looked at Timothy, his large blue eyes flashing in anger. "Your communicators do not work in the sealed room. Anyway, as I was saying, you have all been contaminated and will remain quarantined until further notice in the Great Hall. You can see it through that window," Govenoral Nema said, pointing toward the window on the opposite wall.

"And who are those Chatoobs in that room?" asked Mari, moving to stand next to Kathryn.

Govenoral Nema looked as if he had just swallowed a bug. He sniffed three times quickly. "They are contaminated Chatoobs. We can do little for them." His face suddenly changed back to normal. "You will be pleased to know that the other Federation people are safe. We told them to return to their ship immediately with the news of your exposure to the disease. I'm sure both our governments would readily agree that we do not want any further incidents such as this." He turned to several officers and began talking in a low voice.

Kathryn shook her head. She couldn't believe it. How could they have been contaminated just by walking into a room? "Govenoral Nema," she said, catching his attention. "How could we have been exposed to a disease? All we did was walk down a hall and into a room."

"Ah, yes, Cadet . . . let's see . . . Kathryn Janeway . . . isn't it?" Kathryn nodded. "It is a yellow room you are in, and all yellow rooms are quarantine rooms, Cadet. They are prime breeding grounds for the plague."

"Plague?" she whispered. Govenoral Nema spoke so fast that Kathryn wasn't sure she had heard the word correctly.

"Yes, plague," he repeated, his voice booming around the tiny room. "We call it the Cillian plague."

Kathryn shivered. She had heard of plagues back on Earth, but it was almost three centuries since the last outbreak. She remembered reading about several plagues during the Middle Ages of Earth's history—especially one called the bubonic plague that wiped out about one quarter of the population of Europe. She shivered again.

"Our ship?" said Blinar, his voice shaking and ears still twitching quickly. Kathryn noticed the Tegi was visibly trying to control his temper. "May we talk to the *Tsiolkovs . . . sssky?"*

Govenoral Nema leaned over and listened as one of his officials whispered in his ear again. He shook his head, then turned to Blinar. "In a while, but in the meantime, I must ask you to remove your contaminated clothing, communicators—"

"Our communicators?" interrupted Timothy. "We may need them!"

"We don't know your people and how you react to such events. And we certainly don't want to take the chance that someone will beam out from the Great Hall, exposing my people to the plague, Federation human. Plus, your uniforms, communicators, and tricorders are contaminated and they *must* be destroyed. We will allow you to communicate with your ship with our communications panel inside the Great Hall," he said, sniffing and pointing to the room filled with Chatoobs. "You will change into new clothes now being sent through a tube in the Great Hall. After you change, you will put your contaminated goods in the chute to be destroyed. Food will be provided in the Great Hall at certain hours. We will try to keep you comfortable for as long as possible."

Stunned, Kathryn and the others walked slowly into the Great Hall. The sick and dying were everywhere, and the room smelled like a mixture of pungent cleaning fluid, sweat, and old cooked food. Kathryn had seen sick people before, but never so many all at once—and in such squalid conditions. She grabbed at L'as'wa as the Hassic tripped over a moaning Chatoob male, his face covered with red blisters. "Thanks, Kathryn," she mumbled, shuddering as she continued across the room.

Kathryn noticed that the sight of the sick Chatoob didn't seem to bother Timothy and Blinar. They were easily working their way across the hall toward the tube. But Kathryn had to stop at one point and pull Mari along, his face pale as he stared at the sick Chatoobs around him. Somehow, the cadets all managed to change into their new clothing—each getting a dark brown tunic and baggy pants that smelled of mildew. As they dumped their contaminated uniforms and equipment into the chute, Kathryn balled her fists in anger and sadness. It seemed so unfair. It was her fist starship uniform and communicator, and now it was gone, crushed by a machine on a distant planet.

"Cadet Kathryn Janeway," came the rapid voice of Govenoral Nema over the speaker as the chute closed. "You may call your ship now."

"I believe that's . . . sss my job," said Blinar, moving in front of Kathryn.

Govenoral Nema shook his head hard, his spiked hair waving quickly. And although Kathryn didn't think it was possible, his eyes widened as he pointed a long finger at Kathryn. "No! I said her!" he yelled.

Kathryn put her hand on Blinar's shoulder, then turned and walked to the nearby wall. She hesitated as she looked at the alien communications panel. Suddenly, a three-fingered hand reached over her and pushed two red templates on the panel. It was a tall male Chatoob, his thin face cut by a long blue scar.

"Uh, thanks," she managed to say. Kathryn cleared her throat nervously. "Cadet Janeway to *Tsiolkovsky* . . . Janeway to the *Tsiolkovsky.*"

"Cadet!" came the familiar voice of Captain Wingate. If it were not for the circumstances, Kathryn would have smiled when she saw the captain's face over the communications panel.

"Yes, sir. We have a problem."

"Yes, I heard," he said. "Is everyone all right?"

"So far. But we've all been exposed to some sort of plague. They call it the Cillian plague."

"Doctor?" said the captain, looking over his shoulder. Kathryn watched as Drs. Hess and Tobassa entered into view on the screen.

"Kathryn," said Dr. Hess, frowning and leaning toward the screen. Kathryn noticed even Tobassa looked concerned. "Can you tell us anything at all about the plague?"

"Nothing, Dr. Hess. But apparently, there are plenty of people with the plague in this room." Kathryn hesitated, looking around the room. "In fact, I think some of the people have small blisters on . . ." The viewscreen crackled and hissed, then went blank. "Dr. Hess? . . . Dr. Hess, come in . . ."

"We have lost contact, Cadet Janeway. That is all for now," said Govenoral Nema. He sniffed at them once, turned on his heel, and walked away from the window.

"Goven—" Kathryn tried to say, but Govenoral Nema and his officers continued to walk away. She looked at the others, and noticed she wasn't the only one who was angry. Blinar started to pace back and forth, while L'as'wa, Timothy, and Mari talked together in whispers.

Kathryn hadn't felt this helpless in a long time. *And now that we're cut off from the ship and stuck in this room,* she thought, looking around the Great Hall, *who's going to help us?*

Chapter

5

Kathryn knew why they called it the Great Hall. The room was about the size of the *Tsiolkovsky*'s shuttle bay. It was filled with benches and cots, pillows and blankets, a food table, and a few barrels filled with drinking water—not to mention dozens of sick Chatoobs.

The walls of the Great Hall were dull gray, adding to the somberness of the surroundings. The window that led to the government complex occupied one wall; it also held the communications panel and a camera that monitored the inside of the Great Hall. A food table rested against the opposite wall. A side wall had a long line of cots for the sick Chatoobs; the opposite wall had a sealed door with a tiny scratched and yellowed window, and a single, small crystal window that overlooked the outside of the dome. *This is the closest I've come to the outside of the dome,* Kathryn thought, *and me without my tricorder.*

Grabbing a piece of bread and a cup of water from the food table, Kathryn walked over and sat down with the other cadets on a wooden bench. As she chewed on the bread, she let out a frustrated sigh. For about an hour, she and the other cadets had been walking around the Great Hall trying to ask the Chatoob questions. Many of the Chatoob were lying on cots, their foreheads covered with what looked like a dark powder. Others, even though they were shivering and sick, were trying to clean the hall or tend to the ill. But no matter who the cadets tried to talk to, they were ignored, with many of the Chatoob turning their backs on the cadets. Kathryn felt as if they really *did* have a plague of some kind, and she didn't know how or why.

"I think we should be finding s . . . sssome way of talking with Govenoral Nema," said Blinar, taking a spoonful of a porridge from a bowl. As he chewed, he made a face and looked down his bumpy nose at the bowl. "This tastes like Lojellian grubs."

"What do you have against the Lojellians, Blinar?" asked Mari, biting into what looked like a yellow carrot. "You keep making references to them."

"They are the people who live on the moon that circles . . . sss my homeworld," he said. "We didn't get along too well until the Federation came along. The Lojellians would often trade with the Romulans . . . sss," he said, practically spitting his words, his ears twitching. "And old habits and sayings die hard."

As Kathryn took a sip of water, she noticed an older

female Chatoob wrapped tightly in blankets and lying on a cot. Squinting her eyes, she tried to see the woman's face. She *looked* like the old woman who had disappeared, but Kathryn couldn't tell in the dim light. She stood up and slowly approached the cot.

"Go on farther."

The deep, low tone of the voice stopped her and she felt a hard broom handle between her shoulder blades. When she turned around to face the voice, she recognized him immediately. He was the tall male Chatoob with the scar who helped her with the communications panel. His spiked white hair was shorter than most of the other Chatoob males she had seen, and it moved only slightly as he talked. He wore a thin, black sash around his waist and carried a brown leather pack on his shoulder.

"It is not wis . . . ssse to threaten a member of Starfleet," came another voice. Blinar pushed the broom handle away and stood as close as he could to the Chatoob. L'as'wa, Timothy, and Mari were suddenly standing behind Kathryn.

The Chatoob laughed loudly. "And what do I care about this *Starfleet?*" he replied, sneering at Blinar, his blue eyes opening wide.

"You *should* care," replied Blinar, his eyes squinting.

The Chatoob moved closer to Blinar and pointed to his face with a long, thin finger. "Do you know how I got this scar? It was a short being, just like you, who—"

"Blinar—and whoever you are," said Kathryn, moving between the two, "I think calmer heads should prevail here. We're all in the same predicament, right?" She watched as Blinar and the Chatoob continued to glare at each other. She turned to the Chatoob. "All right. Go ahead. Tell me fighting is going to do any of us any good, and I'll be the first one to do it."

The Chatoob looked at Kathryn in surprise, then turned to the female Chatoob on the cot.

"It's fine, Lane. Let them talk with me," she said, holding her hand out in Kathryn and Blinar's direction.

Kathryn tilted her head. She expected the woman's voice to be weak and feeble, or even for her to talk rapidly like Govenoral Nema. Instead, her voice was strong, soothing, and seemed almost musical, as if no matter what adversity surrounded her, she would always speak that way. Kathryn extended her fingers in the Chatoob greeting. "Cadets Blinar, L'as'wa Ranna, Mari Lakoo, and Timothy Wang," she said, introducing the others. "And I'm Cadet Kathryn Janeway."

"I am called The Zan," the woman replied, moving slowly to a sitting position, not returning the greeting. She waved her left hand in a circular gesture toward her covers. "Please excuse the blankets. The beginning signs of the plague include being cold."

Kathryn felt herself move away from The Zan, then moved back again. "I'm sorry. I-I've never been exposed to a plague before."

The Zan nodded. "This is new to my people, too. We have long been without the plague, but now, like a silent snake in the grass, it sneaks up behind us," she said, twisting her long fingers to move like a snake. She looked wistfully around the room and sighed. "These are

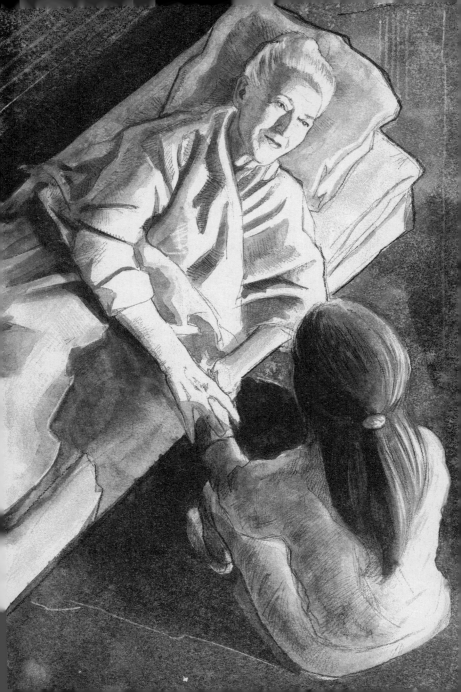

my people, Cadet Kathryn Janeway. I am their leader. And I feel as if I have let them down."

"Leader?" said L'as'wa, puzzled. "Govenoral Nema is leader."

"Yes, of his people," she answered. "We are called the Chatoob, but our people are—"

"Divided into the Chats and the Obers . . . sss," interrupted Blinar, remembering his lesson from the captain.

"Yes, the Obers represent almost half the population. We are the original culture of this planet," she said, clasping her hands together.

"And who should rightfully rule the planet," muttered Lane. Kathryn noticed that he had started sweeping the floor nearby, but was still listening.

The Zan gave Lane a swift look, then turned to Kathryn, suddenly looking tired and sad. "Lane is my second in command. And these Obers around us are the ones who have contracted the Cillian plague. I can only hope the Obers in the other domes have not yet contracted the disease. The plague started in this dome two moontimes ago, and we've heard nothing from them since then."

Timothy scratched his head. "You really don't look different than the Chats. How are the Obers different?"

Lane made a sweeping gesture with his hand. "The Obers speak slowly and with their hands, as the ancients once did; Chats speak as rapidly as the machines they use to speed up their lives. We are simple; they surround themselves with riches. And they sniff the air to show disgust—mostly of the Obers."

"And something you can't see on the outside," added

The Zan, holding up her right hand as if trying to hold
something back. "For some reason, the Obers cannot
resist the plague, but the Chats can." She looked at
Kathryn and tilted her head, her blue eyes widening. "I
truly hope you are all immune. It would not be right for
you to carry such a burden."

"This is really all my fault, Zan," said Kathryn, looking back at the other cadets. "I was following an elderly
woman, and the others just came along with me." She
looked around the room. "And I still don't see her
here."

Lane seemed to almost bark, the biting sound causing
many of the Obers to turn in the direction of the cadets.
"That was no Ober you saw, Cadet Kathryn Janeway."

"He's probably right," The Zan said to Kathryn. "The
woman was a Chat decoy to get you to enter a yellow
room—and contaminate you with the plague." She
folded her arms across her chest and curled over. "Many
of us," she whispered, "including me, were fooled into
following not only elderly women, but sick children into
the plague room."

"But why us?" asked Mari, still looking pale as he
nervously scanned the room. "We were doing them a
favor by bringing in the medical equipment."

The Zan looked up, her wide blue eyes seeming to
burn into Mari. "So that's what you were doing. But
don't you know? It's the government's way of contaminating you in hopes that the Obers are not the only ones
who can catch the plague. They are hoping that your
species will catch the disease just to—"

The Zan turned from the cadets and began to cough

uncontrollably. Pushing Kathryn out of the way, Lane rushed to his leader's side and began to shout orders to several other Obers, his arms waving rapidly. "Can we do anything?" Kathryn asked, looking over Lane's shoulder as he pulled out a bunch of leaves from his pocket and put it on The Zan's forehead.

He shook his head furiously, and Kathryn could tell that Lane was almost feverish himself—with fright. Kathryn looked at Blinar, who shrugged in response. She moved closer to the Ober, helping Lane hold the leaves to The Zan's head. "And what are the symptoms of the plague?" she asked softly.

"First comes a bone-deep cold, like the kind you feel in the middle of snow-time, and along with it a fever," he said. "Then there is fatigue, as if you have been up for days without sleep. The blisters come next, and you don't want to know the rest."

Kathryn saw Timothy and Mari shiver out of the corner of her eye—and could easily understand why.

Chapter

6

It was nighttime, and Blinar, Timothy, and L'as'wa were trying to get comfortable enough to sleep on the hard wooden floor. A soothing light came from two of the Chatoob moons shining in the singular crystal window, but Kathryn didn't care. Mari was lying on a cot, shivering from an unseen cold—the first sign of the plague.

A few hours before, he seemed to be all right. While Blinar stood in front of the Great Hall monitoring camera, Kathryn, L'as'wa, and Timothy tried to take apart the communications console on the wall, but to no avail. Right when L'as'wa managed to pull the covering off the console, Mari collapsed.

Kathryn sat on the edge of the cot and stared down at her shivering friend, remembering Lane's words: *the bone-deep cold, like the kind you feel in the middle of snow-time.* Snow-time on Chatoob was no doubt similar to Earth's winter, and being from Indiana, Kathryn knew the deep bitter cold of that season. Mari, who had lived in the northern regions of North American with his people, the Yupiaq, would know even more about winter than she did. And here he was, shivering in the warm room.

"Don't worry, Kathryn," whispered Mari, looking up at her and trying to smile. "I have my bear with me."

"Bear?" she asked in a low voice.

Mari pulled out a leather string from inside his shirt. On the end was a small, black object. He held it up for Kathryn to see. "This bear. My father carved it. The Yupiaq believe that animals have certain powers. The bear represents strength. So I'll get strong again. I promise, Kathryn, and my bear promises." He put the bear back inside his shirt and closed his eyes.

She smiled and put her hand on Mari's forehead just one more time, hoping the fever would be gone. But it was still there. Kathryn felt powerless—and scared. Would she and the others catch the plague just as easily? All she could do right now was sit and wait and depend on the Chat government, the *Tsiolkovsky,* or just plain luck to pull them through. She wanted to do something—anything—to get them out of there. *If I could just get back to the ship,* she thought, *maybe I could help Drs. Hess and Tobassa find an antidote.*

"Is he feverish?" a deep voice whispered behind her, breaking into her thoughts. Kathryn turned to see Lane, his tall forehead furrowed over his large blue eyes.

She nodded in reply. "He's been this way for about two hours now," she whispered back. "I just thought he was tired at first, and now, he seems to have a fever. I wish I knew more about medicine," she added, frustrated.

"Here, maybe I can help," he said, opening his hands. Lane moved over to Mari's side and took out the pack he carried over his shoulder. Kathryn watched as he carefully unfolded a large white cloth filled with what looked like dried leaves. With his long, thin fingers, he scooped into the middle of the leaves and crushed them into a fine powder along Mari's forehead. "Wilbab. It's a medicine we grow for fevers. The dried plant counteracts the heat of the body. See the heat it absorbs as it touches his forehead?"

Kathryn shook her head. "No, not really. But your eyes can see somewhat into the infrared, and I can only see visible light with my eyes."

"What a shame. There are many wondrous things your people miss seeing," he said, motioning with a sweep of his arm toward the crystal window that led to the outside of the dome. "The seas, the sunrises." He turned back to Mari. "Maybe your friend will respond to the Wilbab as the Obers respond."

Kathryn smiled. "Thank you, Lane," she said, holding out her hand. "I guess we really didn't meet under great circumstances."

Lane took her hand and held on, much to Kathryn's surprise. "It was not you, Cadet Kathryn Janeway," he said. Lane nodded toward the other cadets lying on the floor. "It was that one—the one called Cadet Blinar. He is always trying to take over."

Kathryn knew it was true. Ever since they had become unwilling members of the Great Hall, Blinar was constantly lecturing to the others. All afternoon, he talked to L'as'wa and Timothy, telling them not to give up— that he would figure out how to get them out of quarantine and back to the *Tsiolkovsky*. Kathryn noticed that neither cadet really listened. "Like all of us, Blinar is a first-year cadet," she whispered to the Ober. "None of us has too much off-world experience, and Blinar likes to think he's in charge. He wants to be a captain of a starship one day."

"I have been listening to him talk to the others. His are promises with no results. That is more like the actions of one who is scared," he said, releasing her hand and putting the dried herbs back in his pack. He looked down at Mari. "I will check him later. Now I must see how The Zan is doing."

Kathryn watched as Lane moved smoothly and quietly through the other sleeping Obers toward The Zan. The older Ober was still awake but did not seem to be any better. Every now and then, Kathryn would see the covers around The Zan's cot start to quiver and she knew the Ober leader was feverish again.

"Kathron," said L'as'wa, pulling at Kathryn's sleeve. "It is my turn. I will watch Mari. You have been watching for two hours."

Kathryn nodded and tried to smile at the Hassic cadet. "Thanks, L'as'wa. I wanted to walk around for a while— see if I can pick up any information. I can't just sit here.

Mari's not getting any better. We have to do something." She looked around the Great Hall. "And I think I know who can help us."

Kathryn slipped through the cots and stood next to Lane. She watched as he carefully put Wilbab on The Zan's forehead and nodded to Kathryn. "She rests."

"Good. Lane, I need your help."

"My help? I am sorry, but I only follow the orders of The Zan, Cadet Kathryn Janeway," he said, holding his right hand out toward her, then turned back to the shivering leader.

"Even if it may mean helping her?" Lane looked at Kathryn, his eyes seeming to flash even in the dim moonlight. She could see that she had caught his attention. "We were trying to reach my ship by modifying the communications panel on the wall, when Mari got sick. Now maybe you can help."

"How?"

"You showed me how to use the communications panel when we first arrived. You must know how—"

"Very little, Kathryn," he said, hesitating. He made a small circle in the air with a long finger and smiled. "But I do know something about how the backup communications are installed."

Kathryn woke the other cadets and explained her plan. As Blinar and Timothy talked in front of the monitoring cameras, Kathryn, L'as'wa, and Lane worked on the panel. Lane pointed to several wires, while Kathryn and L'as'wa rerouted the pathway circuits. "Try it now," said Lane, pressing a panel. L'as'wa held several wires up from the wall, then nodded to Kathryn.

"Here goes." She pressed the two red templates on the panel. "Cadet Janeway to the *Tsiolkovsky* . . . Cadet Janeway to—" Suddenly the panel sent out a high-pitched hum. "Look out!" she yelled. An explosion sent sparks flying into the air!

Kathryn covered her head and hit the floor. As she fell, she heard Lane and L'as'wa also fall hard to the ground. As the panel continued to explode, some of the Obers ran from their cots and mats—their arms flailing wildly and many of them screaming. Kathryn felt like screaming, too. The room was in chaos, and several Obers fell to the floor, pushed by others trying to get away. Even Kathryn was kicked in the leg by an Ober running to the other side of the room.

As the noise slowed to a few hisses and pops, Kathryn looked up. Most of the Obers were in a group against the far wall. They were hugging each other and trying to move as far away as possible from the explosion, while Timothy and Blinar tried to calm them down. Lane was grabbing the side of an empty cot, pulling himself up slowly. L'as'wa was on her knees, coughing from the smoke. As Kathryn pushed herself to her knees, she saw movement in the far window.

Standing there was Govenoral Nema and three of his officials.

Govenoral Nema pointed to the communications console on the wall, his long spiked hair waving rapidly. He sniffed once and turned to Kathryn, quickly mouthing the words, "Too bad. We'll fix it as soon as we can." He turned on his heel and walked away.

"I bet," she muttered, gritting her teeth. She realized

that the Chat government was not helping at all. She brushed off her hands, then looked up at the broken, smoking console. Split wires hung out of the wall, and soot covered the top of the panel. Even the monitoring camera was broken and burned.

L'as'wa crawled over to Kathryn. "Kathron. That panel. It should not have exploded. Believe me."

"I know," she whispered back, pushing some hair off her forehead. "I think it was booby-trapped. Someone doesn't want us to contact the ship—or get out of here." But we're going to fool them, L'as'wa. We *are* going to get out of here."

Kathryn drummed her fingers on the floor. First, they were cut off from the ship and now they were cut off from talking to the Chats. She may be only training to become a science officer, but that didn't mean she had to sit around like a Lojellian grub, to use a saying from Blinar.

She knew something had to be done, even if it had to be done one step at a time. And *she* was going to do it.

Chapter

7

It was toward morning, and Kathryn noticed that Govenoral Nema was taking no chances: A guard now walked past the large window every ten minutes, no doubt the result of the broken monitoring camera.

Most of the Obers were asleep—thanks to Lane's words and hand gestures soothing them. But Kathryn was too restless to relax. "That's it," she whispered to herself, standing up. "I'm sick of not knowing what's going on." Slipping quietly around several sleeping Ober children, she made her way toward The Zan's cot.

"Zan?" she whispered urgently, sitting down on the side of the bed and leaning toward the older Ober. "Zan, it's me, Kathryn."

The Zan looked up, her large blue eyes glassy from

the fever. "You must find a way out," said The Zan, waving her left hand wildly. She grabbed Kathryn's hands with her long fingers. "You must get away. There is a cure for the disease. A sea grass, along the oceans. But they won't let us leave the dome. No one is ever let out of the domes." The Zan let go of her hands. "The Chats found the Cillian plague again and sent it through my people," she whispered.

"But—" Kathryn started to ask.

"It's Govenoral Nema," she said, staring into Kathryn's eyes. "He and the other Chats want to get rid of my people. We were once part of the government, but the Chats took over. They don't want us working our way back into the government." She lowered her voice, speaking quickly and urgently—almost like a Chat. "But, Kathryn, some of my people have escaped to the outside and are in hiding. Not all of my people believe it, but many of us know the air is clean outside the domes, and there is plenty of land for all of the Chatoob. The Chats want to get rid of the Obers who know. So they kill all of us so the Chats will continue to believe the air outside the dome will kill them. They want to control their people under the domes."

"But what's the point of contaminating us with the plague?"

"If the Federation thinks Chatoob is a plague planet," said The Zan weakly, "they'll give more technology and help to the Chatoob government to find the answer. I can imagine Nema is ecstatic now that he has contaminated you. That way, the Federation will send aid even faster. Nema is not a stupid man, Kathryn. With more technology, he has more power."

The Zan started to cough again, a ragged sound that came from deep inside her chest. She raised her hands in the air, then folded her long fingers across her chest, curling into a ball on the bed. Kathryn started to panic. She had heard that sound before: lungs filling with fluid from infection. She remembered the same sound coming from her sister, Phoebe, when she was only five years old—her sister sick with bronchitis. Kathryn's family had gone backpacking for several days when her sister started to cough. Her father had insisted that the family rough it, so they had no communicator or location device. She remembered the grueling seven-hour walk out of the nature preserve, each of them taking turns carrying Phoebe through the thick forest—all the while, her sister coughing.

Kathryn was startled by someone yelling and pulling on her shoulder. "Just what are you doing," came the deep voice of Lane. "Can't you see she's ill?"

"I'm sorry. I was just—"

"Snooping around," interrupted Lane, his eyes flashing. He gestured with his hands toward Mari's cot and the other cadets. "Just like your friends. I've been watching all of you. And I don't care what The Zan says— I'm beginning to think you are all spies!"

Lane pulled Kathryn up roughly, forcing her to stand.

"Hey, I was just—"

"You were what?" asked Lane, his usual soothing voice quivering with rage. "Did Nema send you to spy? Or is the great Federation really working for Nema?"

Kathryn pulled her arm away from Lane, but he was still able to hold her hand in a tight grip, his three long fingers twisting all the way around her hand. "We are not spies," she said, turning her head so she could stare into the wide eyes of the tall Ober. "We just want some answers."

Out of the corner of her eye, Kathryn saw The Zan push herself to a sitting position. She made a weak circle with her hand, then called out to Lane. "Lane, Kathryn is not a spy. You have my word." Lane's grip lessened on Kathryn's hand. "I told her about the sea grasses, Lane. It's the only way."

Lane held The Zan's gaze for a moment, then turned to look at Kathryn. She could see the torment in the Ober's mind. He nodded quickly and released her hand.

The Zan lowered herself on the cot and closed her eyes. "Somehow, Kathryn, you have to get outside. Gather the grasses from the sea. To save us. Please."

Kathryn forced herself to smile. "Don't worry, Zan. I'll find a way."

It was the middle of the night. Kathryn didn't feel like sleeping and neither did the other cadets. For most of the day, they sat on the floor near Mari's cot, talking quietly about how to escape to the outside, but they couldn't agree on a plan. Blinar and Timothy were whispering back and forth, while L'as'wa played with several small wires and metal pieces from the blasted communications panel she had hidden in her jacket. "What are you doing, L'as'wa?" Kathryn asked.

"Communication is important," the Hassic whispered.

"I can make a crude communicator. We may use it somehow."

Kathryn nodded and looked around, half listening to the others. She was frustrated, wondering what her father would do in a situation like this or what he would expect her to do. She knew she should face this problem one step at a time. But what was her first step? And not only that, she noticed that L'as'wa's hair was still as perfect as the first day she saw her. *Now I know I'm feeling sorry for myself,* thought Kathryn, sighing.

"I just can't believe this," Timothy was saying. He leaned his head against a wall. "I spent my entire life wanting to join Starfleet Academy. I even did my solo shuttlepod flight when I was sixteen just to qualify. And now look—on my first mission, I'm quarantined from the universe."

Blinar snorted. "I know what you mean, Timothy. I wanted to be the first Tegi in the Federation and show my father that he was . . . sss wrong," he said, almost in a whisper, "that the Federation people were really better than he thought. Now I may not get my chance."

Kathryn looked at the Tegi. It sounded like Blinar had the same problem she did. Her father always won the arguments—when she saw him. So there was a reason for Blinar's pompous attitude. Maybe she was translating his enthusiasm for Starfleet as arrogance, or even that he was scared. Though she tried not to think about it, she was scared, too. "Listen," she said finally, leaning toward the others. "Let's go over this once more. Mari is getting sicker. It could be the plague or even the flu."

"Or maybe that weird carrot he ate," added Timothy, scrunching his face.

"Whatever. None of us has the medical background to tell," Kathryn answered. "But it may mean we *can* catch the plague. And as each one of us gets sick, it gets more difficult to escape," she added, looking over at L'as'wa, "not to mention that we don't know how you and Blinar will react to the plague."

"And your suggestion?" whispered L'as'wa.

Before Kathryn could answer, she heard a strange moaning noise. L'as'wa nudged her and pointed to the sealed door on the far side of the room. In the dim light, Kathryn could see a lone Ober muttering softly over a wrapped body, sometimes rocking back and forth, sometimes gesturing with his hands, as he spoke his ceremonial chant. As Kathryn and the other cadets watched, the man pushed on the sealed door on the far wall. As the door slid open, the Ober placed the wrapped body on a slab inside, then stood back. There was a whirling noise, and smoke from the other side of the door covered the body. The Ober chanted again for about a minute, and when the smoke cleared, the body was gone!

As the chanter walked back to his cot, the door sealed shut with a quiet hiss. Kathryn looked at the others, her eyes wide. The cadets stood up and walked quietly over to the door, L'as'wa looking through the door's small, yellowed window. "He is gone. I do not believe in magic, Kathron."

"Me neither," she whispered, taking her turn to peer through the window. "Bodies just don't disappear. There's something familiar . . ." Kathryn stood back from the door and snapped her fingers. "I know. I read about it just recently in one of our history books. Didn't Captain James T. Kirk meet up with something like this? On the planets Eminiar Seven and Vendikar? The people were at war for five hundred years but used no weapons. The attacks were launched mathematically by computers. When the citizens were declared 'casualties,' they would voluntarily report to disintegration chambers. Maybe these people are being disintegrated, too."

"Such chambers have certain sounds. A certain look. Not this chamber," said L'as'wa.

"And I thought I saw the slab move," added Timothy. He peered through the small window. "And look—on the other side of the slab."

Kathryn moved to look inside the chamber again. Across the room was another small door. "An airlock, I bet! So they aren't disintegrated."

Blinar nodded. "An airlock is a perfect way to make a body dis . . . sssappear."

Kathryn looked through the small window again just to make sure her eyes weren't playing tricks on her. For the first time since they ended up in the Great Hall, she felt hopeful. "Cadets? We needed an escape plan, and I think we may have found one."

Chapter

8

"You went into the chamber?" asked Lane, staring wide-eyed at Kathryn and Blinar. His right hand gestured in a circle at the chamber, then fell to his side.

"No. We just looked in the window after . . . well, after the body disappeared," she explained. "And, Lane, we saw what looked like an airlock on the other side of the chamber."

Kathryn glanced at Blinar. "An airlock could be the key to our es . . . ssscape," Blinar added.

Kathryn continued, not allowing the Ober to get a word in. "Here's my plan: Mari will play 'dead.' L'as'wa rigged up a primitive communications device from the wall panel pieces. So after we slip him into the chamber and he gets outside, he'll contact our ship. They'll come and get us, then use everything in their power to help your people find a cure." She took a deep breath, waiting for his response.

Lane closed his eyes and bent his head. After a few seconds, he opened his eyes even wider than usual and looked at Kathryn. "The chamber is off limits to us. It has become a sacred place and I fear no one will go along with your plan. But if I explain that it may help find a cure for the plague, maybe they will understand." He stood up slowly, almost as if he were tired and worn. Kathryn noticed he shivered as he walked over to a group of Obers. *The start of the plague,* she thought, shaking her head.

Kathryn and Blinar walked over to L'as'wa and Timothy, who were standing near Mari's cot. Timothy leaned over the sick cadet. "Mari, old buddy. Are you sure you want to go through with this?"

"Count me in," he said, his teeth chattering. "I get wrapped in blankets so I'm warm. I get a communications device so we can talk. And I get to magically disappear. It can't be any worse than riding a dogsled with only one dog in the middle of a blizzard, right?"

"Or facing Lieutenant Muldov's Planetary Exploration final exam," Timothy joked, smiling at his friend.

L'as'wa dug into her pocket and pulled out the crude communications device. She attached it to his dark tunic. "You talk to me. I talk to you. The circuit is always open. Contact the ship, too."

As they wrapped Mari in several sheets near the chamber door, all sorts of questions were going through Kathryn's mind. After all, it was risky. Would the Obers stop them? Does the airlock really lead to the outside or are government troops waiting on the other side? Would Mari be able to contact the ship? She also wondered how she, as a simple scientist, ever managed to get into this position.

Several minutes after they finished wrapping Mari in the sheets, Lane walked up to the cadets. "As I thought, no one likes your plan."

"But why?" asked Timothy, looking down at his wrapped-up friend. "Mari's willing to sacrifice—"

"The Obers do not want to escape. They are sick and weak. And they feel they may contaminate their own people if they leave the Great Hall," Lane explained, folding his long fingers in front of him as if he were tired. "But they will allow Mari to pass beyond the chamber. I will help you." He reached over and touched several light colored squares on the wall panel's round pad. "There. I just reported Mari's 'death.' While we wait, I must chant." As Lane began the ceremonial chant and hand gestures over Mari's "body," Kathryn looked over at Blinar. She could tell he was nervous—his ears were twitching from time to time. L'as'wa and Timothy were huddled together, occasionally whispering.

Kathryn jumped visibly as the sealed door opened. Each cadet grabbed a corner of Mari's blanket and lifted him. "Watch the merchandise," Kathryn heard Mari whisper loudly.

Blinar frowned and pulled on his side of the blanket. "Shhhh . . ."

Carrying the "body," the cadets moved toward the open chamber. As they lifted him onto the slab, Mari's sheet caught on the table, causing L'as'wa to stumble. "Sorry, Mari," the Hassic whispered.

Kathryn looked around quickly. "Let him down easy," she said, lowering her side of the blanket.

"Oomph!" said the blanket.

Timothy looked up at Kathryn and tried to smile. "Should I kick him?"

Kathryn shook her head at Timothy. "No, he may yell again. And he's our only ticket to the outside."

"Nothing like feeling used," moaned Mari in a low voice.

"Shhhhhhh . . ." responded the four cadets around him.

Lane chanted and the cadets retreated back into the Great Hall. As they watched, smoke covered their friend's body. A minute later, the smoke was gone—and so was Mari. Moving slowly, the cadets turned and walked back to an empty corner of the room, trying not to disturb the Obers. "Mari!" L'as'wa whispered urgently into the communications device. "Talk to me!" The device clicked twice.

"Ooof!" came the response. After a few seconds, Mari continued. "Yeah, I'm fine." Kathryn grabbed L'as'wa's arm and smiled. Timothy almost shouted out loud, but Blinar held up his hand. "I'm almost unwrapped. . . . I'm trying the ship. *Tsiolkovsky* . . . come in. Captain?" Static burst out of the device.

Kathryn held her breath. "Mari? Mari!"

". . . here, Kathryn," he answered, his voice fading in and out. "The ship is beaming me up. It worked . . . you go . . . but . . ."

The device went dead. They all looked at each other, stunned.

"Now what?" Kathryn noticed that Timothy's voice had a touch of panic in it.

Kathryn knew how he felt. They knew that Mari had made it outside. Did the government officials find him? Was he beamed up to the ship? Or was he still out there, cold and ill with no help from his friends? Kathryn thought of how this was her plan. Was this what it was like to be a leader—to make the decisions and maybe lose one of your team? She felt almost sick to her stomach.

"I think we should go after him," she finally said, her voice firm with determination. "The guard walks by every ten minutes. We can time it so we enter the chamber after he passes, then hop into the open airlock."

"How do we know where to go from there?" asked Blinar, looking skeptically at Kathryn.

"You still have me," said Lane, walking up to the cadets. He shivered slightly as he continued, his arms at his side. "I'm not afraid to be outside the dome. I was out there once and lived to tell tales about the adventure. We could look for Mari. And we could also go find the sea grass that will help my people. I know the Obers outside the domes know how to process the medicine. We can contact them."

"Good idea. But not you, Lane," L'as'wa protested. "I have been watching you. You show signs of the plague."

"It's only the beginning. I'm still strong. And after all," he said, turning to Kathryn, "who else can pick out the correct grasses from the sea?"

Kathryn hesitated. "All right," she whispered to Lane, then turned to the others. "And I'll be the body this time."

"No, I want to be," protested Timothy. "Kathryn. Mari's my best friend. If I sent him out there and something went wrong . . . Well, it's the least I can do right now."

Blinar snorted, his ears twitching at Timothy. "I would make a better body."

"No," said Kathryn. "Timothy's right. So far, the Chats think only humans can get the plague. So let's give them another human."

As they prepared Timothy, Kathryn looked around. Everywhere the Obers were whispering to each other. Many times, their voices would raise and their hands would gesture almost furiously toward the cadets. But still, no one stepped up to offer their help. According to Lane, they were all too sick with the plague—too weak and scared to run and fight.

They wrapped Timothy in a short time, and just after the guard walked by, Lane began the chant. Kathryn watched as the chamber opened. Lane put Timothy's wrapped body on the slab—and slid inside. Just as quickly, Kathryn, L'as'wa, and Blinar slipped into the chamber, just as the room filled with smoke. With a hiss and pop, the airlock door opened. As Timothy's wrapped body slid off the slab, the others plunged through the open airlock door right behind him.

The airlock door slid shut, then hissed as it was sealed. Kathryn crouched down next to Timothy and motioned to the others to do the same. Suddenly, the air inside

the small chamber changed dramatically: It was no longer stale and warm, but it was wonderfully refreshing and cool. Kathryn took a deep breath, her head clearing with the fresh air.

And just as suddenly, the floor dropped out from under her!

Chapter

9

Kathryn grabbed at Timothy, trying to cushion him as they fell into a long, twisting chute. She could see the others trying to grab at the sides of the metal slide—all trying desperately to slow their downslide speed, but to no avail. Even though she wedged herself between the sides of the chute and Timothy, her friend would still occasionally let out a cry. She knew it must be even more scary for Timothy—he was wrapped in the sheet and couldn't see what was happening.

She fell out of the chute with a thud, her hands stinging as they hit the grassy ground. As she looked up, she saw Timothy rolling away from her. She stood up quickly and raced over to her friend. "Timothy! Are you all right?" She unwound the sheet frantically from around his head and chest as he tried to sit up.

"Next time you have an escape plan, Cadet Janeway, count me out," Timothy said, holding his head as Kathryn continued to pull at the blankets.

L'as'wa, rubbing her arm, knelt down beside Kathryn and Timothy. "He sounds fine," she said. "Still obnoxious as ever."

Kathryn nodded. "How about you?"

"I hit my elbow when we landed," she said, looking at her arm. "I fell on a stone. It will be fine."

Kathryn looked around. In the dim moonlight, she could tell the others were shaken, but all right, too. Blinar was standing up next to Lane, scanning the horizon. "I don't s . . . sssee anyone—Mari or otherwise," Blinar called back to Kathryn.

She looked at L'as'wa. "Does the communicator work?"

L'as'wa shook her head. "I don't understand. It should work. Mari said he was beaming up. All I get is silence."

Kathryn sighed in frustration. "Are you sure—"

"Enough talk," said Lane, gruffly. Kathryn looked up at the Ober and noticed he looked different. His eyes were wider than usual and he made no gestures with his hands when he spoke. As she watched, he moved his pack from side to side, as if it were uncomfortable. Maybe the plague was catching up with him; or maybe he thought they would be caught. He yanked on a thick, straight branch of a nearby tree and tested the heft of the stick in his hand—an action that almost looked like a threat to Kathryn. Lane turned and pushed by the cadets. "Follow me."

* * *

Kathryn was soon tired of walking over the dusty, dry terrain. *I think I'll make a mental note,* she thought, *next time I'm in a fix like this, I'll ask how far it is to the sea.* This was definitely much worse than backpacking in the wilderness with her family. At least she had water and food at that time, even though her backpack weighed about thirty pounds. Here, they had nothing, except a few chunks of bread they had saved from their last meal.

She also noticed the others were tired, too. The thin-soled shoes provided by the Chats were uncomfortable on the uneven, sandy ground. Even Lane looked tired and would often shiver as he walked. Kathryn stole a look at L'as'wa and shook her head. "I keep telling myself one step at a time. But it's still hard."

"I know. I hope we get there soon, Kathron. We are all tired."

Lane paced as the group stopped to rest near an open glade. "Just one working communicator," muttered Blinar. "Just one little phas . . . ssser. Why couldn't we be more like the Klingons? I heard they carry many weapons at all times . . . sss. Why don't they teach us something like that at the Academy?"

"Cadets?" said Timothy, as he leaned against a rock. "All those in favor of Blinar keeping quiet, please raise your hands."

Kathryn and L'as'wa raised their hands.

Blinar grimaced. "Before I stop talking, I have one question. Why hasn't the *Tsiolkovsky* picked up our pres . . . sssence yet? If Mari did beam out like he said, shouldn't they be picking us up, too?"

No one had an answer. Kathryn was puzzled, too. Certainly the captain would have someone monitoring the planet at all times. Maybe someone was blocking their signal. And even though Kathryn tried not to think of the worst-case scenario, it still popped into her mind: Was the ship still in orbit?

Lane struggled up a sandy hill and waved to the cadets behind him. "Here it is!"

Kathryn reached the crest of the hill and smiled. She had never seen such a wonderful sight: It was sunrise, and they had traveled to the edge of a beautiful blue-green sea. As she listened to the sounds of the waves washing on the shore, Kathryn felt tired. If only she could curl up on a soft, sandy dune and allow the gentle waves to soothe her to sleep.

Lane walked to the edge of the sea. Stooping down, he put long fingers in the water and pulled out some long, red blades of vegetation. He looked over at Kathryn and smiled, his blue eyes suddenly wide with excitement. "It's still here. Can you see the heat coming from it?" Kathryn shook her head. "That's right—you can't. Believe me, Cadet Kathryn Janeway, it looks wonderful to my eyes. And there is enough of it to process. Come, Cadets. All you have to do is pull out the grass at the base, but only if it's bright red. Try to keep out the blue ones. They're not ripe enough yet."

Kathryn walked to the water's edge. Everyone took off their shoes and rolled up their pant legs. They were soon gathering the vegetation, carefully placing the sea grass into Lane's pack. As the water washed up and over

Kathryn's bare feet, she wished she could enjoy the feel of the warm water. But she had work to do.

L'as'wa took a deep breath. "It is good air here, Kathron."

"And I think I'll build a house here," said Timothy, looking up at the sand dunes as he picked the sea grass.

Blinar shook his head as he scooped up another batch of grass. "First you want to es . . . ssscape from here, now you want to build a house."

Kathryn bent over, listening to her friends and smiling as she washed a bunch of red grass in the warm water. Suddenly, Lane was standing next to her, his eyes watching not the ocean, but the land. "Is that it?" Kathryn asked, looking at Lane's full pack.

"Yes," she heard Lane answer.

Kathryn stood upright—to face a hand phaser Lane pointed at her. Her heart froze even further when she saw Lane sniff the air twice.

Before she could say anything, the Ober whistled three times, the noise shattering the peaceful sunrise. Kathryn's heart pounded faster as she saw some movement over the short rise of dunes: Running toward them were the silhouettes of seven tall forms. As they came closer, she could see they were government officials, each carrying blaster rifles in their arms. Thick protective suits covered their braided uniforms, and gas masks sheltered their faces.

"Blas . . . sst!" Blinar hissed. He looked up at the guards and threw a bunch of grass into the shallow water. "Kathryn—quick! We have to—"

Kathryn put a hand on Blinar's arm, stopping him

from making any sudden moves. "No, Blinar. Not now. We're outnumbered."

The guards quickly surrounded the cadets. No one spoke as they pushed Kathryn, Blinar, and L'as'wa together. One of the officials nudged Timothy, and he pushed the guard back. As the guard brought his rifle up to strike Timothy, Lane called out, "No! Govenoral Nema doesn't want any of them hurt."

As a guard pushed Kathryn past Lane, she stopped, noticing that he didn't seem as sick as he did in the Great Hall. She also realized that Lane was probably the reason why Mari's signal disappeared and the *Tsiolkovsky*'s sensors had not found them on the planet—the government was blocking the signal. "Tell me one thing, Lane, whose side are you really on?" she said, hoping the sound of her voice was as biting as she felt.

Lane threw his head back and made a whistling sound. "You really didn't think that I was going to help you, did you?" he said, talking almost as rapidly as a Chat. "I am the perfect spy. The Zan's right hand? She offers me nothing," he said, spitting and whistling again. He leaned over almost nose-to-nose with Kathryn, his wide blue eyes trying to stare her down. She didn't flinch.

"She'll find out when we get back to the Great Hall, you can count on that," she said, still glaring at him.

"I don't think so," he said, standing up straight, his long fingers grabbing a blaster rifle from a nearby guard. "They are taking care of her even as we speak. And me? The government has promised me a cure if I turned you in—so Govenoral Nema can make an example of you," said Lane, almost hissing his words as he sniffed at the cadets. Kathryn shook her head when she noticed his spiked white hair waved slowly. "And maybe they'll even give me a position in the government." He pulled a gas mask over his head and motioned to the others. "Take them back to the Great Hall!"

The cadets were pushed along quickly, retracing their steps back toward the dome they had just left. As they walked, Timothy caught up with Kathryn. "I feel a little funny," said the cadet, shivering. "Kind of cold." Kathryn's eyes went wide. She put Timothy's arm over her shoulder and helped him to walk.

Her anger kept her walking the long distance back to the dome. She was furious and she couldn't help it: Her plan to help the Obers and the others backfired, because the man she and The Zan had trusted had betrayed them. And now, Timothy may be coming down with the plague.

She was also scared—afraid none of them would make it off this planet alive.

Chapter

10

L'as'wa landed next to Kathryn as she was thrown unceremoniously into the Great Hall. Kathryn grabbed her friend's hand and pulled her to her feet. "Thanks," said L'as'wa, brushing off the arms of her tunic. "I joined the Academy to be a navigator, Kathron. Not a backpacker. My feet are killing me."

Kathryn nodded in agreement. Her feet were hurting, too—especially because she helped Timothy through the dunes and back to the domes. Blinar was tending to Timothy now, and from the look on her friend's face, she could tell he wasn't doing well.

"Do you see The Zan?" she asked L'as'wa.

The Hassic looked around the room, squinting her

eyes to see in the dim light, then shook her head. "You do not think they—"

"I don't even want to think about it," interrupted Kathryn. "Let's ask around."

Kathryn and L'as'wa walked over to a group of Obers near the food table. As they approached, one of the Obers looked over, her eyes wide with fright. The others turned, too, and moved away as the two cadets approached. "Hey, wait," Kathryn said, grabbing the last retreating Ober by the arm. The man let out a cry and pulled his arm away. "I just want to ask about The Zan."

"They won't listen to you."

Kathryn looked down at a young Ober, a female that couldn't have been more than seven. "What do you mean?"

"They're afraid of you," she said, swinging her arms in a wide circle. "You followed the one called Lane to the outside of the dome. And after you left, that mean man took The Zan away."

"What mean man?" asked L'as'wa.

"You know," she said, looking down and pulling at a bandage on her hand. "One of Nema the Meany's guards. I don't like him."

Kathryn smiled at the youngster. "Did they say where they took The Zan?"

"No." And just as suddenly as the young girl appeared, she ran, disappearing into the crowd of Obers.

Blinar walked over to Kathryn and L'as'wa. "Timothy is . . . sss resting. And I have an idea, Kathryn," he whispered, leaning close to her ear. "Why don't we use the same way out of the dome to es . . . ssscape?"

"I don't think so, Blinar. Thanks to Lane, they probably already know that escape route," she said. "What we have to do now is to rally the troops. Blinar? L'as'wa? Follow me—and follow my lead."

The three cadets marched over to a large group of about thirty Obers. As the group started to disperse, Kathryn held up her hand. Many of the Obers stopped and turned. She took a deep breath, trying to stop her heart from racing. *I sure hope this works,* she thought. *I've trained too hard to give up—especially to get into the Academy. I will get back.* "I know you are all concerned about our walk outside the dome," she said out loud. "But there is no need to fear the outside of the dome. The air is safe, and we will not contaminate you with anything else."

"You don't know what it's like," yelled an older male Ober, his thin fingers twisting quickly as he spoke. "First the plague, and now you come in, contaminated with the outside air. Who knows what horrible germs you carry?"

Several Obers in the group muttered, agreeing with their kinsman. Kathryn continued. "Believe me, we don't carry any germs! Listen," she said, pointing to Timothy, "another one of us may be suffering from the plague. You and he need help—help we can only get from my starship. But we can't contact them without *your* help."

"We help you escape," said a young female Ober holding a child, "and we are punished while you disappear in your ship."

Frustrated, Blinar leaned over to Kathryn, his ears twitching slightly. "This isn't working, Kathryn," he whispered. "Come on, we'll figure s . . . sssomething else out."

Kathryn looked at Blinar and shook her head. She couldn't—no, she *wouldn't*—quit now. She was too close. "As someone once told me, Blinar, one step at a time. We need their help," she said, then turned to the Obers again. She was amazed at how calm she was, even with the Obers angry stares. "As you can see, we have been outside, and we are not dead from the air."

"You will be," an Ober yelled from the back of the room. Several Obers gestured with their long fingers held outward toward Kathryn.

"Really? Well, then there's something else you should see." Kathryn ripped the shirtsleeve on her left arm and held up her hand. "You all know what this is, don't you?"

Her wrist-watcher was still there, the bright yellow Tana flower looking as fresh as the first day she wore it. She smiled as several of the Obers gasped.

Following her lead, Blinar and L'as'wa also held up their left arms to the crowd, their wrist-watchers still a vibrant white. Several Obers moved closer to the cadets. "I know you're all mad, and you should be mad," she continued, lowering her arm. "The government has given you this plague, lied to you, and now they have taken your leader! But we can help you, if you help us."

One of the taller Obers walked out of the crowd and faced Kathryn. "I am known as Bana, and I have fought with The Zan for ages." He turned to the others. "Has this disease taken the fight out of all of you? Do you not remember the Collector of Tobatten? We were able

to change the law for our people. And why? Because
we stood up to the government. And who was at the
head of the fight? The Zan."

"But what of the other Obers?" asked an older male
Ober, clasping his fingers in front of his chest, his wide
blue eyes staring intently at Kathryn. "We will contaminate our people!"

"Maybe," added Kathryn. "But you said you cured
the plague years ago, and my ship will help you find the
cure again. All your people will be cured." Kathryn
looked around the Great Hall. It was so quiet, all she
could hear was the whimpering of a young Ober lying
on a cot behind her.

Several of the Obers began to talk and gesture among
themselves. Finally, two older male Obers walked to
Bana and made two large circles with their hands. Kathryn smiled, realizing that circles made by the Obers was
a good sign.

Bana turned to the cadets. "Several of us are strong
still, even though we carry the plague. We will help.
What do you have planned?"

"A massive escape," Kathryn answered. "We can attack the guards all together. The shear numbers will help
get us out of here. Then we can contact my ship and
find an antidote."

"Then we must fight until we reach Nema's office,"
he said. "That is where the central communications are
located. You can contact your ship from there."

"Do you think your people are strong enough to fight
off the guards?"

Bana nodded. "Some of them will need to stay behind.

But most of us will go. We will help you, Federation Cadets, but on two conditions."

"Yes?" she said, folding her arms across her chest.

"In the future, you will speak highly of us who are killed in the escape," he said, holding his left hand toward her. "And second, you will not let the Obers die out forever," he said, his wide eyes becoming wider.

Kathryn nodded. "You have my word."

Chapter

11

Kathryn had never seen such a rush of people in her life.

Bana and another male Ober had started a make-believe fight just as the guard walked by the window on his ten-minute routine pass. Kathryn had banged on the glass, trying to get his attention. The guard wasn't going to take chances—two more guards came before Kathryn heard the door hiss open.

The three guards had no chance. They were knocked out cold as dozens of Obers pushed their way, running and yelling, out into the dimly lit corridor. As the Obers ran, they picked up anything they could use as a weapon—broken pieces of tile or wood, and some even carried metal bowls from the Great Hall. Kathryn was amazed at their strength even though they were suffering from the plague—and even the ailing Timothy seemed to be caught up in the push to escape.

Bana and the cadets were in the back of the pack. Blinar eventually found a weapon: an old, unlit torch stick leaning against a wall. He turned and yelled to Kathryn. "You and the others . . . sss stand behind me. And have that sheet-rope ready. We may need it." Kathryn noticed his ears twitching madly, his brown hair matted to the top of his head. She nodded, her hand squeezing the makeshift rope on her shoulder that they made from old bedsheets.

Bana turned to Blinar. "I can see heat from the guards. They're coming up from behind!" he yelled.

Kathryn and Blinar ran to the opposite sides of the hallway, allowing the others to run through. Finding a hook on the lower part of a door, Kathryn put the rope through the loop, then tied the line into a tight knot. She threw the other end of the rope to Blinar, and he, too, looped the line around a hook low on another door. As he finished tying his end of the rope, Kathryn pulled. She nodded to her fellow cadet—the rope was taut enough. *That should trip them up for a while,* she thought, looking back at the rope in the gloomy corridor.

The cadets continued to run down the hall, following Bana and the other yelling Obers through several twists and turns. Suddenly, the Ober stopped and pointed down a hallway to the left. As she and the other cadets watched, the running Obers overwhelmed two more guards standing in front of an ornate wooden door. Bana looked at her and smiled, then made a small circle with his hand. "We present to you Govenoral Nema's council chambers. You will no doubt find him there, along with the central communications panels so you can contact your ship. I can only hope news of our escape was slow in reaching him. We will be outside, guarding the door for you."

Kathryn and the others quickly ran up to the chamber doors. The wooden door was ornate, with the typical braid of gold, green, and red all around the edge of the doorframe, but it had no doorknob or handle. Timothy shivered, then pointed to a panel on the wall. "It looks as if that's our only way in," he said. L'as'wa touched a few of the strange symbols in various sequences. "Let's see, if you were to . . . try a binary sequence . . ." Timothy said, wiping his forehead as he helped L'as'wa, ". . . no, use the coding manifold bypass . . . there, that should do it." The door *whooshed* open.

Blinar was the first to rush into the chamber, stopping in the middle of the room. Timothy and Kathryn quickly followed, while L'as'wa ran for the communications panel along the side of the chamber.

Kathryn watched as a surprised Govenoral Nema stood up, then suddenly changed his mind and sat back down. A sickening smile formed across his face as he touched a panel on his chair with a long finger. "It's no use, Federation Cadets," he said in his usual fast speech, sighing and leaning back in his seat. "A noble effort indeed, but too late. I have summoned my guards, and you have no weapons. I believe there is a game on Earth called chess—and the final move is checkmate." He turned to Kathryn. "Checkmate, Cadet Kathryn Janeway."

Kathryn swallowed her anger. "I used to be very good at chess, Govenoral Nema. You can't say checkmate until you're sure your opponent has made his or her last move. My countermove to yours? I know that the Obers are the only ones who can catch the plague." She watched Nema nod, still with that maddening smile on his face. "Maybe that's true, but how about me? I'm not an Ober. Maybe I carry a different strain of the Cillian plague. Oh, and not to mention—I've been outside."

She watched as Nema squirmed in his seat. Before he could speak, L'as'wa walked up to the front of the Chat's desk and lifted up a long, frayed red wire. "You are good at stalling, Kathron," she said, nodding to her friend. She turned to Nema. "Excuse me. Your Govenoralship? Is this something of importance?"

The govenoral's face turned white. "Where . . . where?"

"This?" L'as'wa said, holding up the wire. "I found this wire. In the wall unit over there," she said, pointing in the direction of the comm link. "This leads to the panel on your chair. Does it not?"

Kathryn could have hugged L'as'wa at that point, even if she was being melodramatic. She walked closer to the govenoral's desk. "Now we talk terms, Govenoral Nema. Without the guards."

The govenoral shifted in his chair. Kathryn didn't know if Chats could sweat, but from where she stood, she thought she could see beads of sweat breaking out on his tall forehead. "You have nothing to offer me," he said, looking up at Kathryn and still trying to smile. "You really have to stop trying to escape. You'll spread

the plague to other Obers in the population, you know. I'm sure you don't want that on your conscience. So when the guards get here, just cooperate and go back to the Great Hall with the rest of the Obers."

"The Obers . . . sss escaped with us," hissed Blinar, with a satisfied smirk on his face.

Kathryn thought the govenoral flinched just a little. He stared at the Tegi, then stood up slowly. "How dare you spread this disease to my entire population. Is this the way your people work? And we want to negotiate to join your Federation?" he said, throwing the words rapidly, almost spitting out the last word.

Kathryn shook her head. "Nice speech, Govenoral Nema. But you can't intimidate us like you do the other Chats and Obers. Your government has done nothing to help find the cure for the Obers—only to hinder." She hesitated as she remembered her promise to Bana. "Now we're here to contact my ship so we can save the Obers."

Kathryn turned toward the communications console. L'as'wa was working furiously, trying to establish contact with the *Tsiolkovsky*. She slammed her fist on the console in frustration. "It is no good, Kathron. This comm link is being shielded."

Kathryn turned to Nema. "And I imagine the entire planet is being shielded from our ship." She smiled, knowing now where the *Tsiolkovsky* stood: There were no negotiations going on between the ship and the Chatoob government. Otherwise, there would be open communications.

The govenoral shrugged. "And? I still won't help you. I would rather—"

"There!" cried L'as'wa. "I broke through!"

Before Kathryn could say anything, there was a commotion outside the door. Govenoral Nema smiled as about a dozen Chatoobs in dark blue outfits and gas masks ran into the room, pointing blaster rifles. Kathryn felt as if all her strength were drained away. The Obers had been overrun. *And we needed just a few more seconds,* she thought, watching the troops surround the room.

Govenoral Nema turned to Kathryn, a smug look on his face. He pointed a thin finger at the cadets. "Arrest these criminals!" he shouted.

But the guards turned their weapons on Nema. The last two guards to enter the chamber carried no weapons. "If anyone is to be arrested, it's you," the guard on the left said in a calm voice, hands gesturing in a grand circle toward the govenoral.

Nema's face dropped and he sank slowly into his seat. "The Zan," he whispered.

She tore off her gas mask and bowed slightly to Nema, then waved to the guards. "The Obers thank your guards for their uniforms." Lane was standing next to his leader, peeling off his gas mask. He turned to Kathryn and smiled, but she was not about to return the favor.

Out of the corner of her eye, Kathryn saw Timothy push his way toward Lane, his face contorted with anger. As she started after the cadet, Timothy yelled to The Zan. "Don't get near him," he cried, pointing to Lane. "He's a traitor, Zan, he's the one who turned us in!"

Kathryn was still a few yards from Timothy and The Zan. The Ober woman merely smiled and reached out for the ailing cadet. As Kathryn watched in horror, Lane took out a long instrument from his leather bag. In his three long fingers was a hypospray.

As fast as she could, Kathryn ran straight toward Lane, grabbing at the hypospray just before the Ober could push it into Timothy's neck.

Chapter

12

The Zan looked at Kathryn's hand holding Lane. "Not now, Lane," she said, moving a finger in three small circles. As he lowered his hand, she turned to Kathryn, her wide blue eyes calm. "I understand, Kathryn. And I admire your courage. You are trying to protect your fellow crewmate, much like I try to protect my own people."

Before Kathryn could reply, a familiar whine filled the room. She watched as Captain Wingate, Doctors Hess and Tobassa, and several security guards suddenly materialized—and Mari Lakoo.

"Mari!" yelled Timothy, trying to turn.

Kathryn was never so happy to see anyone in her life. She almost rushed over to the now-healthy cadet to give him a hug, but she stood her ground. Before anyone could say anything else, Dr. Tobassa raced over to Timothy, nodding to The Zan. "Good job! You made it, Zan," he said in his booming voice, patting her on the shoulder.

Dr. Hess ran over and threw open her medical case. "Did you inoculate him?"

"Not yet," The Zan responded, still holding on to Timothy. "Lane was just going to give him the inoculation, but—"

"Well, come on now. What's the holdup?" Tobassa said, reaching for a hypospray unit. "These are busy cadets. They don't have all day."

Kathryn tilted her head, still standing next to Timothy and The Zan. "I'm afraid I'm missing something here."

Captain Wingate walked up to Kathryn. "Mari made it back to the ship, thanks to your plan. Then the Chats shielded the planet from all communications and scans. But since Mari was carrying the plague, Drs. Hess and Tobassa were able to isolate it and provide an antidote. Then, while we were trying to break through the shield, Lane contacted us on your communicator."

"How? It was destroyed," Kathryn said.

"No," said Lane, his hand circling toward the govenoral cringing in his seat. "Nema lied to you. He told you it was destroyed. He wanted to keep the technology and use it to his advantage."

"And he did, too," added Dr. Hess. "He called us several times on Blinar's communicator and said you were all suffering greatly. And then asked for more aid."

"After I left you outside the dome," continued Lane.

"I was able to convince a Chat to tell me what happened to your clothing and equipment—and to bring me a communicator. It's amazing how you can bribe people, especially when you tell them you've been outside. When they fear for their health or their family's health, they'll do anything for you."

"The planetary shield wasn't too strong, so Ensign Hader worked out a way to concentrate the transporter beam so it would cut through the shield. We tried it out by beaming down some of the antidote to Lane. And because he had the run of the complex," explained the captain, "we asked him to try and find you. Then we could beam you out one at a time. As it was, you had already escaped. Lane didn't even get a chance to contact us when the shield around the planet disappeared."

"That was L'as'wa's doing. She broke through the shield just as The Zan came in," said Kathryn, smiling at her Hassic friend. "But, Lane, you mean all that was an act outside—with the troops?"

Before he could answer, The Zan broke in. "Yes, it was the only way I could think of to contact your people. We would help each other. We knew where you were, and your ship could help us process a large amount of medicine. We knew the Chat government would not harm you—you mean too much to them."

"So you used us . . . sss?" said Blinar, shaking his head.

"I believe we all 'used' each other," she said, turning to the Tegi cadet. "Did you not convince the other Obers to fight their way out of the Great Hall so you could escape and go for help?"

Kathryn stood straight. "That was my decision. I take full responsibility."

The Zan turned to face Kathryn. "And it was a good decision. It is what saved my people and helped us to catch Nema." Her voice lowered and she folded her thin fingers in front of her chest. "We're both leaders, Kathryn. And leaders must protect their people by making some tough decisions. You made many decisions in the past days—and you were successful. I also made decisions. But we both did it to help our own people. And now, may I help your friend?" she added, nodding to Timothy.

Timothy looked over at Mari. His friend nodded, and Timothy nodded eagerly at the Ober leader. "I'm ready, Zan."

Kathryn looked into her eyes and gave a quick nod. The Zan pushed the hypospray into Timothy's neck, the instrument hissing as it released the medicine. Kathryn looked at the Ober leader. "I guess I'm next."

As Drs. Tobassa and Hess continued to inoculate the other cadets, Lane turned to Govenoral Nema. "And what about him?"

"I'd like to take care of him," said Tobassa, releasing a hypospray into L'as'wa's neck. "Starting a plague—I still can't believe it." The Chat cringed as the big doctor glared at him. Kathryn thought Nema must be terrified to be in the room with so many people who knew about his treachery.

"And so, Cadet, what are the allegations?" asked the captain, turning to Kathryn.

She took a deep breath and stood in front of the

govenoral's desk. "I can't even begin to tell you all the allegations that should be brought against you," she began, trying to sort through the past days in her head. "First, you've held back the fact that the air outside the domes is fine for breathing—just to control the population. You've also illegally contaminated your people with a disease, held Starfleet personnel hostage, destroyed Federation property, and worst of all, tried to annihilate a culture you're governing."

A noise across the room caught Kathryn's attention. "Kathron. Eliminate destruction of Federation property," L'as'wa said, standing next to an open cabinet. She stood back, revealing five Starfleet uniforms and four communicators wrapped in clear plastic bags.

"Skip navigation—you'd make a better detective," Mari said to L'as'wa.

The captain turned to Govenoral Nema. "As Federation authority on this mission, I am hereby withholding any more humanitarian aid to your planet. The charges are obvious, including the kidnapping of our cadets."

"This is absurd—"

"I think not," said Kathryn, moving closer to the desk. "Your list of crimes is even longer than that—just ask the Obers."

"Captain," said The Zan. "Based on the rules of our people, I hereby take over as the provisionary govenoral of the Chatoob government." The Zan hesitated as Nema sputtered in the corner of the room. Kathryn looked at the Ober in surprise. She hadn't realized that the fall of the Chats would mean the Ober would rule. *What will become of the Chats?* she suddenly thought.

"*All* the people of Chatoob are now my first priority," the Zan continued, almost as if she had read Kathryn's mind. "I would like to request that the medical team from your ship help to inoculate the rest of the Obers. That is all we ask. Then you may be sure that we will take care of the problems of our own planet."

Captain Wingate stared at The Zan. "I'm afraid kidnapping is a serious offense where we come from."

"And here, too, Captain," replied The Zan. "But I don't think your system of government would have the power to punish the corrupt Chat government officials for their crimes. Here, we can. And be assured, we will."

The captain nodded to the Ober woman. "All right. But we will have to resume negotiations with your people at another time. I must talk with the Federation about what has happened here and make a full report."

"Of course. Before we can negotiate anything with the outside universe, we must make sure our own house is in working order." As Kathryn and the others listened, The Zan's hand gestures became almost mesmerizing. "We know that the Federation cannot do anything about the government, but I and my people can. And while we're at it, we will tell all of our people about the richness of the land, seas, and air outside the domes. We will use the great dome structures as reminders to never allow our environment to get so bad that we are driven into the domes again. And of course, as a reminder of how a government can lie to its people. Thanks to your cadets, there is new hope for Chatoob. It will happen. Just give us time, Captain."

Kathryn smiled at the older Ober. "I wish I could be here when that happens."

The Zan laughed, a rich laugh that filled the room. "Captain. I also have another request." Captain Wingate looked up. "I would like Cadet Kathryn Janeway to be in charge of the team that brings the additional antidote to my people," she said, still smiling at Kathryn.

"No problem," answered the captain, smiling proudly at the cadet.

"And, Captain," The Zan added. "You must also watch out for Cadet Kathryn Janeway. I can tell that she will be after your job someday."

Kathryn took the Ober's hand in hers. "Just give me time, Zan. I have to take it one step at a time." The Zan nodded and squeezed Kathryn's arm. Letting go, she made three large circles with her right arm in salute—then turned, ordering the Obers to accompany the still sputtering govenoral to the prison.

As the progression of Obers left the room, L'as'wa walked up behind Kathryn. "What are you thinking about, oh, leader of the day?"

"Who, me? Oh, nothing really," she said, smiling at her friend. "Just about a ladder. In fact, I think I'll call it Janeway's ladder."

About the Author

Patricia Barnes-Svarney leads an enjoyable "double" life: One minute, writing nonfiction science books and articles, the next minute, science fiction—for both young readers and adults. She wrote *Star Trek: The Next Generation: Starfleet Academy: Loyalties* and two *The Secret World of Alex Mack* books—*Junkyard Jitters!* and *High Flyer!* Her hobbies include reading, astronomy, birding, herb gardening, and hiking. She lives in Endwell, New York, with her husband—writing and trying to keep all the wildlife in her backyard fed. You can contact her at svarney@ibm.net.

A Special Event!

Celebrate the Klingon™ Day of Honor with Worf and Alexander!

STAR TREK
DEEP SPACE NINE®

#11

DAY OF HONOR
HONOR BOUND

To lose one's honor is the greatest loss of all...

By Diana G. Gallagher

A MINSTREL® BOOK

Published by Pocket Books

1393-02

Sometimes, it takes a kid to solve a good crime....

Original stories based on the hit Nickelodeon show!

#1 A Slash in the Night
by Alan Goodman

#2 Takeout Stakeout
By Diana G. Gallagher

#3 Hot Rock
by John Peel

#4 Rock 'n' Roll Robbery
by Lydia C. Marano and David Cody Weiss

(Coming in mid-October 1997)

To find out more about *The Mystery Files of Shelby Woo* or any other Nickelodeon show, visit Nickelodeon Online on America Online (Keyword: NICK) or send e-mail (NickMailDD@aol.com).

A MINSTREL BOOK
Published by Pocket Books

1338-02